Henry Copley Greene, George H. Hallowell

**Plains and Uplands of Old France**

A Book of Verse and Prose

Henry Copley Greene, George H. Hallowell

**Plains and Uplands of Old France**
*A Book of Verse and Prose*

ISBN/EAN: 9783337371937

Printed in Europe, USA, Canada, Australia, Japan

Cover: Foto ©Andreas Hilbeck / pixelio.de

More available books at **www.hansebooks.com**

# PLAINS·AND·UPLANDS OF·OLD·FRANCE A·BOOK OF·VERSE·AND·PROSE BY HENRY·COPLEY·GREENE

SCIRE
QVOD
SCIENDVM

BOSTON·1898
SMALL·MAYNARD & COMPANY

# To K. S. C.

WHOSE SPIRIT ALWAYS NEAR MY THOUGHTS
BRIGHTENED MY HAPPINESS IN SCENES THAT
SHE WOULD LOVE

H. C. G.

*Among the Pines*
*Dublin*
*New Hampshire*
*August 22*
*1898*

# CONTENTS

vii

# Plains and Uplands of Old France

## THE YONNE AND THE SEREIN

THE Cathedral of Sens dwindled, lopsided, among huddling brown roofs, and as my bicycle whirred me on through the morning mist two rows of shadowy poplars, now near, now far, followed the lonely Yonne. But straight as a glance the road led on through wheatfields and endless vegetable patches where peasants were at work, while toward me on the road peasants came jogging along in market wagons or in carts laden with rolls of bark.

"Good morning," said I.

No answer. The drivers stared at me in silence, and their horses were glum. Each donkey, however, turned toward me a kindly interested ear. So on I sped, cheered past many a round white post proclaiming Paris more distant. Then after long, imperceptible climbs and short rushing coasts I caught up with a procession of trees that glittered in the early sunlight, and at last, passing under the arch of an old gate-tower, I came, through Villeneuve-sur-Yonne, out over the river into lands unkempt.

There no *route nationale* sped arrow-like along the valley, and pointed with scornful blue signs to villages left aside. Rather a communal road meandered among worn kilometre stones and past a desultory dull green sign, up the slope, to a group of low houses. Among them, as I slowly jostled over the cobble-stones, a woman dragged her child to shelter. From an oblong brown puddle beyond, ducks eyed me askance. Again in the ensuing fields lank sheep-dogs, blunt-nosed and rough-furred, but mere bundles of nerve for all that, greeted me with unfriendly surprise. But the shorn flock, unperturbed, barely interrupted the busy rustle of their munching; only a lamb or two looked up — to sneeze.

Peacefully, then, through grassy fields I came to hamlets that even the communal road

# Plains and Uplands of Old France

ignored; and so, with my imagination still lit
by their church windows, surfaces almost
trembling with burning vibratory points of red
and purple, I again crossed the dreaming, rush-
invaded Yonne, and pushed on to where
Joigny rises from its bridge to a steeple-
crowned hill-top.

Though silver-gray in the enchanted distance, and picturesque as some river-sketch by
Turner, Joigny at close range was dusty, dull,
provincial. In it, to be sure, there stood a few
ancient houses, and among them wandered little girls whose heads were wreathed with white
for the first communion. Through the streets,
too, a cart paraded pompously from corner to
corner announcing with blare of trumpet and
rattle of drum, that tickets might already be
bought for a stupendous theatrical perform-
ance to take place that evening. Impressive,
again, was the coachman who waved me past
his yellow waistcoat and superb green trousers
into the hotel. But like all else in Joigny he

betrayed my hopes; a mere maid led me up two staircases and around a court-yard gallery to the one thing perfect in Joigny, its den of *commis-voyageurs.*

In the bare dining-room they were feeding, many and wonderful; and in their midst, at ease beneath a stuffed boar's-head, the greatest of them all, the veritable Type, sat wiping out tumbler and plate with his napkin. Then he tucked it into his collar, and sniffed at his bread; gorged, complained of the condiments which his giggling wooden-faced Audrey added to the meats; at last, picking his teeth with a yellow-handled pen-knife, "shut up in measureless content."

Of such was Joigny.

Joigny, however, was for me but a gateway to untainted France. For after the midday meal and long lazy communing with Le Petit Parisien I whirred on through cool breezes and along flat roads, among bachelor-buttons and bright poppies. Happy hints for the colorist

# Plains and Uplands of Old France

these blossoms seemed; and when after quiet
hours I lay atop the only hill on the road and
munched wild strawberries under a rose-bush,
I fell to dreaming of a vague field-spirit clothed
in flame and jewels stolen from French wild-
flowers and from Gothic windows. "Which
were more dazzling?" I questioned; but for-
got all questioning as I woke in the light of
sunset to whir down toward silent Auxerre.

The gray church-towers, just tinged with
pink, slowly mounted above the horizon hills,
then disappeared. Houses darkened the street
and garden-walls hemmed it in on both sides.
But it turned; I came steeply between sweet-
scented acacias to where long canal-boats on
their way toward the Rhone rested on the tree-
shaded river. Thence up again, following a
narrow street, I passed under a straddling,
gay old Renaissance clock-tower, and wandered into the cathedral square.

Through a door in the darkening great fa-
çade, then down a step or two, I went into a

5

pillared aisle where a few old women knelt in mute prayer. Dimly above them floated infinite calm. In distant heights the mystery of unseen color glowed among the arched shadows. Time merged into mystery. The air was still, but a tiny yellow flame appeared among the pillars, and nearer and nearer along the stones came the clapping sound of *sabots*. There was a clanking of keys, and a high nasal voice echoed through the vaults:

"*On ferme les portes.*"

One by one the worshippers rose. The door slammed, reverberating behind them.

"*On ferme les portes.*"

Then I too went out and the cathedral key was turned behind me.

The calm night, a vague reminder of the upland quiet to which I was returning, gave place next morning to gay mockery. Outside my window washerwomen jeered one to another; and when I looked out over their washtubs

# Plains and Uplands of Old France

only the half-felt influence of the church across
the court held their tongues decorous. As it
was, one greeted me with a loud *"nom d'un
nom!"* while I rubbed my eyes and looked
sleepily at the tower of Saint Eusèbe. A dear
Romanesque tower it was, so stumpy and
quaint that I marveled at the cock-sure van-
dalism of the old builders who had smothered
it in Gothic work. How cheerily they were
applauded, though, by the two gargoyles, one
mock-devout with ears lying back on his
calmly folded wings, the other with ears almost
a-wag as he grinned in the face of the sky. So
malevolent was he that as I came at last into
the street the very sun caught his spirit, and
shone down on each commonplace citizen with
truly cynical candor. Even in the cathedral it
revealed a lack of rich fineness of detail. But it
left the proportions of the large building impressive, while to the glorious choir windows it
gave the life of brilliant colors in harmony.

Alive, then, with many a bright impression,

# Plains and Uplands of Old France

I left Auxerre behind and by a long winding ascent came into fields delightfully untilled. Bright under the sun's rays waved wild grasses; on the water-shed rocks showed brown through broken ground.   All things were vigorous and untamed.   Even the sheep-dogs seemed clad in rougher fur as I sped by toward the valley of the Serein.   So down I coasted gleefully, my shoe thrust brake-fashion against the front wheel; then on through vineyards and a village, I came at noon into Chablis, the town of white wines.

There, after the solitary conviviality of lunch, I sat on a sunny bench watching two old houses with balconies quaintly overhanging the river; and as I watched in digestive calm, a cat eyed me from the opposite shadows.

Suddenly she stiffened; for she had seen what I now saw, — an ancient hound coming nearer and nearer. The cat crouched trembling.   The hound, looking neither to the right nor to the left, passed by intent on duty.

# Plains and Uplands of Old France

Kitty sighed with relief. But the regular *flop flop* of the hound's paws had hardly faded into the distance when a woolly small pup came prancing along the pavement, *clickity click*, most gaily. 'Sdeath! The cat, flattening herself against the wall, slid gracefully to a place of vantage. The wool-dog pattered past. All was well. But suddenly out of the corner of his eye he spied her. She sped; he followed. She disappeared down a cellar window, like a cork swallowed by a whirlpool. Just in time the wool-dog stopped, bracing himself back with his forelegs. So for a moment he stared woefully into the depths, then glanced up and down the road. No one in sight. "My discomfiture has not been seen," thought the wool-dog, tossing his head in the air. And proudly he pranced along the hound's path, kicking out his toes before him and hitting the pavement with his nails, *clickity clickity click*.

"French dogs, after all, like French men care only for effect. At last the reality is known,"

# Plains and Uplands of Old France

I cynically told myself, and triumphed over the woolly pup while I mounted my bicycle and wheeled on beside the smooth Serein.

For a time I triumphed unpunished. Showers, to be sure, pricked the surface of the river; but between sprinklings the fields, glittering refreshed in the sunlight, tinged the air with the moist perfume of new-mown hay and the rich sweetness of purplish and deep-red clover. I basked in the pleasure of it. But as I walked my bicycle up the steep hill of Sainte Vertu, — or was it winding Sainte Colombe? — a peasant met me with a taunt.

Reining in his horse, he called down to toiling me, "That bicycle does n't go *plon, plon.*"

Somehow the sound imitated the quick, regular motion of pedalling so well that I mounted my bicycle in great shame and puffed up the incline, seeking admiration at the top. There, however, two big turkeys, with necks and heads aflame, glanced at me coldly and made throaty, insufferable remarks. I ignored them.

# Plains and Uplands of Old France

But then a flock of geese, beaks open and tongues stuck out stiff and straight, followed me down the road hissing. This was unbearable! Turning upon them I hissed back. And though they raised their chins and turned away with a look of indifferent contempt, I am sure they were deeply mortified. But now dogs began to rush out at me barking ruthlessly. Among them a huge long-haired nondescript, with yellow eyes and a gray terrier-like head, made a furious onslaught on my right leg which automatically doubled up, like a bird's leg among the feathers, ignominious.

I was abashed and punished. No matter, no one had seen me, thought I. So proudly, like the wool pup following the hound, I pranced my bicycle on past where the Serein disappears in a wooded ravine; received the smiling " Good days " of roadside children ; at last safe in friendly little Avallon, dismounted content, where a spaniel with forelegs crossed in sweet gentility lay dozing before the Red Hat.

# Plains and Uplands of Old France

## GÉRARD DE ROUSILLON

*GÉRARD, the holy man of wars*
  *Whose love of heaven and hate of hell*
  *Drove out from France the infidel,*
*Slept deep with Bertha 'neath the stars*
  *While angels sang.*

*For Bertha and good Count Gérard*
  *Had labored with the laboring throng,*
  *And borne great beams and stones along*
*To build Her shrine whom, from afar,*
  *The angels love.*

*Before the dawn good Count Gérard*
  *Awoke to pray with Bertha there;*
  *But she was gone, and in despair*
*He thought her false, as maidens are,*
  *To vows of love.*

*In anger, then, the man of wars*
  *Sped swift his dewy path along.*
  *He found her building while a throng*
*Of angels aided, and the stars*
  *Her praises sang.*

# Plains and Uplands of Old France

## VÉZELAY

HAT? You depart already?" asked Jules as I came out of the Red Hat into the morning sunshine.

" Friends await me," said I.

The gay little cook tapped his club-foot against the pavement, turned his moustache high up at the ends, and shaking his white-capped head asked slyly "Dey are Laydees?"

"Hardly," I answered, thinking of old acquaintances, Philippon, the laughing Vézelay sexton, and Gauthillot, mine host.

But as I rode off Jules proudly repeated the significant word "Laydees," and showed his white teeth through a crescent-shaped smile, and shook his finger at me in mock condemnation. Evidently he meant his joke to echo in my mind all the way to Vézelay.

Only a street or two off, however, my memory of his voice faded and was lost in sweet tones which vibrated faintly in the air and, as

13

# Plains and Uplands of Old France

I came to an arched doorway, grew into soft singing. Strangely ethereal it seemed. But when I passed through the door, the old church harmonies rose still more ethereal. For beyond a white grating that shut out even the priests and acolytes, nuns stood among their wreath-crowned little charges, chanting alone; their voices, pure as the unearthly spirit of their lives, rose to heights mysteriously finer than the glory of far greater voices, and drawing near in the spirit to Saint Bernard and the childlike Count Gérard, made the chant like a star at dawn, silvery with a star-like radiance still bright from the mediæval night.

Filled then with the ancient happiness that survives in Vézelay, I came from the nun's chapel along a grass-grown empty street, past the twisted columns and richly-carved arches of Saint Lazarus' church, and down into a valley which turning the flank of a hill suddenly became a mountain gorge.

On each side turreted gray and purple rocks

# Plains and Uplands of Old France

broke out from the soft foliage, and below, just beside me, there hurried a broad stream, first marked with swift streaks, then ruffled and foaming, again smooth. Its speed raced me along through the dampened air, now in bright sunlight, now in the shadow of pines, and still triumphant in its vitality, switched me aside into the dust of wayside Pontaubert. There, in the porch of the Templars' church, swallows looked out cheerily from their nests of mud; and two stone lions, presiding over the village fountain, greeted me with suave dignity. Alas, the chin of one was daubed with blue paint. Imagine it, a blue chin in the presence of the Templars' shades! Poor lion, as I sat in the calm of the undisturbed old church I sympathized with him deeply. Yet, I reflected, he was only a late Renaissance lion; probably he looked down on a Romanesque church with a Gothic narthex, and didn't at all care to be pitied. So, callous to his plight, I wandered further by meandering roads.

# Plains and Uplands of Old France

At last, in a bit of woods, I met two very peasant-like sisters of charity, and asked my way.

"Straight ahead," they answered, "Go straight ahead, and you will see Mount Vézelay there on high."

There indeed, next moment, I saw the conical fortified hill and the two familiar church-towers standing dark against the glare of sunset, while the little river Cure, fringed with bushes and poplars, sang brightly beside a squad of tile-roofed houses and beneath the bridge of Saint Père.

How musical the shining stream had been to float in, summers ago, beneath the blue sky! That memory brought me hurrying toward it, and a glance at the towers carried me across and half way up the hillside. There, however, a donkey and I stopped and stood still to greet each other ; so, till the peasant-girl in his cart woke with a loud "Ai! Va!" That drove us both forward so speedily that soon,

# Plains and Uplands of Old France

very soon, a bare plastered house, the inn, welcomed me with its window-full of coffee-pots and bottles. And at the doorway the kindly hostess greeted me, then leading the way through the tiled entry, pointed to Gauthillot himself in white apron lording it over the great open fire and the kettle on the crane.

"Would I not come into the garden?" he asked, abandoning his chickens and the gossiping neighbors. For his roses, he assured me, were mine; so also were the strawberries, all I could eat.

This I knew from experience. What was better, I remembered, host and hostess, sexton and postman were always ready to chat. The very animals were companionable. At many a meal of mine, "Gauthillot Junior," the turnspit, beat his tail against the floor in carnivorous longing or despair. His enemy the hound often stared through the window at my mutton. Once a wandering horse even put his head in to snuff the cream-cheese. Only the ducks were indifferent, and without a glance waddled in single file to the duck-pond.

As for me, generally alone in the little dining-room, I dreamt of old battles and visions. At times, however, a stranger arrived; and feasting together we conversed about the hateful Prussians or about the country whence I came.

"Are the monkeys and crocodiles very terrible in the swamps about Boston?" asked a sympathetic farmer.

But an amateur of painting, the venerable father of the curé at Avallon, discoursed on "that infidel Darwin," orthodoxy and angels. "Only grocers, retired grocers, scoff at their doings," he used to exclaim, and so would stray into tales of mediæval Vézelay and of Gérard its founder.

Like some other heroes of the days before the Franks became French, Count Gérard de

# Plains and Uplands of Old France

Rousillon was half sainted. For not only did he rule wisely his own land of Burgundy, but as guardian of the young King of Provence he drove the Saracens from the south, and on the Seine, where the church prayed "From the fury of the Northmen, Good Lord, deliver us," he defeated those pagans. But before he could attain complete goodness, he was to suffer. Charles the Bald quarreled with him about the ownership of Sens. And in vain Gérard and his nephews, Fourques, Séguins, Gibers and Booz fought most valiantly. With his wife, Bertha, Gérard was forced to take refuge in the Ardennes where as a mere charcoal-burner he learned gentleness and humility.

So after seven years of trial and of communion with a friendly hermit, Gérard and Bertha came at last into their own.

But again the devil filled Charles with envy so that he began another war. Now, however, Gérard defeated him in Flanders and near Soissons. A third time they fought at Pierre

# Plains and Uplands of Old France

Perthuis near Vézelay. Droon, Gérard's father, unhorsed the Count of the Ardennes. But the Count rose and stabbed him. "Montjoye!" cried the French. "Saint George!" cried Fourques, Séguins, Gibers, Booz and all the Burgundians; and they fought like lions till the river Arsis ran red. Even to this day it is called, La Cure, "Cuère, a heart bleeding with dolor and torment." "Behold the ground covered with dead," said the pitiful Gérard. "I am very certain that men will curse us, and against us the beasts will roar to God."

After twelve victories, when the king had fled to Montargis, Gérard and his dear wife thankfully founded twelve monasteries, the greatest of which are Pothières where the relics of Gérard and Bertha have worked many miracles, and Sainte Madelaine on "Mount Vézelay which fears no assault."

Such was the beginning of Vézelay, and from its beginning came much of its charm. Yet that was perhaps more an imprint of later

# Plains and Uplands of Old France

glories and sufferings. So I thought as I wandered in the twilight past remnants of a church whose doors had once been barred with the symbolic briar against the oppressed serfs of this fief of the Holy See. So it seemed as I walked on outside walls that had defied the king; and so I thought again as I looked down into the spreading valley whence, years after, Saint Bernard had driven thousands, shouting, "God wills it! God wills it!" to attack Jerusalem. But when finally I came to Sainte Madelaine, huge and silent below the new-born silvery stars, the kind naïveté of its founders, Gérard and Bertha, seemed to fill all Vézelay with their sweetness.

So humming a monastic song in their honor I stood still, and dreamily the while watched a glow-worm whose steady greenish light illumined the grass about him long into the night.

But after all was it this that I had come to see? Hardly, thought I as I was waked next morning by the contented *grung-grung* of sows and the mingled lowing of cattle.

Under the window was the country fair, a great square of cream-colored cattle and of peasants in blue blouses. And in the early sunlight there rose over all a pleasant clattering hum that tempted me toward gossip of wheat-crops and wines. So down I came into the swarm. But eager again to be in my favorite haunt, Sainte Madelaine, I soon wriggled my way to the steep village street.

"Good morning," said a gentle voice, and I nodded to Madame the bakeress standing before her windowful of big loaves.

"Good morning," I returned, and trudged on. A little higher, opposite a cobbler's door where sabots were drying in the sun, the postman greeted me genially; next moment I was trudging on past the butcher's stone house and past a gentle building on the carved lintels of whose windows was carved in old French,

Like to a Dove I will avoid all blame
And I will make my manners like my name,

# Plains and Uplands of Old France

and further, past windows opening on Gothic vaults, I came finally to the summit of the hill and the little square before the abbey-church.

There I never stayed; for though the almost Byzantine effect of the rich triple doorway is stirring, the second story of Gothic sculpture jars. Indeed the calm gravity of the early building appears only in the sides. There the walls and heavy buttresses are stern; almost too stern, they seem, in contrast with the leering faces under the eaves. But when, that day, I entered the long side door and looked along the aisle, its infinite succession of round arches, of columns and broad wall surfaces filled me with kind delight in their lovable color-harmonies of blushing pink and green-gray, deep red-brown and fawn color, united one to another by the felty texture of the stone.

As "the mediæval one," an occasional travelling companion of mine, sententiously affirms; "the grave beauty of faith is nowhere in France more perfectly embodied." But

23

faith, it seemed to me, was not the only mediæval feeling embodied in these stones. And
even the sexton, jolly, dimpled Philippon of
the twinkling eyes, saw that the old artisans
had expressed half barbarous passions also;
for now as besplattered and dusty from his
vineyard he wandered with me in the aisles,
he pointed out a strange long-haired demon
leering down from a capital.

"It is the demon of voluptuousness," he
said, crossing himself and laughing, "See, he
is tearing the woman's flesh. Sainte Madelaine pray for us."

The idea of Sainte Madelaine, added to
Philippon's permanent pride in the church,
put him in mind to show me the crypt once
more. And after leading the way through
long aisles, he lit a little candle and went first
down the stairs. — "Heads!" said he.

I ducked and came into the low twilit
chapel hewn deep in the rock. Here had been

the shrine where Louis and where Richard Coeur de Lion had knelt, for here in their time had lain the body of Mary Magdalen. Yes, Lazarus had been bishop of Marseilles; Martha had tamed the terrible horned dragon of Tarascon; Madelaine, after converting Provence had rested at Saint Maximin and for Count Gérard had been brought hither. " But the Protestants, the Protestants," Philippon went on gravely; "they dragged her out and had burnt her. They also broke the carvings on the outer door and smashed the head of Saint John. Indeed they were little better than Prussians."

" Take care !" he called; suddenly ducking at the doorway he blew out the candle; and again we were in the choir aisle.

There stood Philippon, his head bobbing up and down like a red apple on a wind-blown tree, and chattered. There were so many things that he liked to talk about and show. One must know Vézelay, he said. He would

go again with me onto the glorious windy
terrace behind the church and point out the
rampart to Quarré-les-tombes where men
worshipped Saint George and where a thous-
and graves were miraculously prepared for
Gérard's soldiers; he would point out the
Morvan mountains; if I were willing he
would guide me up the tower and in the gallery would show me old sculptures.

I was very willing, for among them is a
blessed Virgin, with peasant's face indeed, but
almost Greek in its regular outline, and of
such sweetness that it seemed to incarnate the
very spirit of Vézelay.

Yet the charm of legendary Vézelay, vivid
though it was in the church of Sainte Madelaine, sank dim at last behind the present.
Gradually, one Sunday morning, as the church
benches were filling with women and children
and with men in their cleanest blouses, all
former worshippers drifted away toward vague

and shadowy times. And when the comfortable priest, with his two lay assistants and a bevy of boys, came in procession down the nave, my visions of monks and crusaders passed into final darkness. The imagined clanking of knightly armor died in the actual notes of a Gregorian chant. And where the pale Saint Bernard had once passed, there now marched up the aisle two robed peasants, one singing gently, the other bellowing false notes in a voice rough as his untamable white hair.

To him, and to the rest of Vézelay, church music seemed hardly more sacred than it is to singers in the blasphemously Parisian Madelaine ; for as the procession neared the altar he spat twice unconcernedly, and no one seemed surprised. What is more, the very sexton, unholy Philippon, later urged the bread on me, a heretic. "Won't you take some — just a tiny piece?" he begged; and when I refused, the massive peasant next me

seized a handful which he munched content-
edly through the rest of the mass.

"This" thought I, "this is the true spirit
of Vézelay!"

But when mass was over Philippon, with
the *clopety clop* of his sabots echoing in the
vaults, led me through a little side door into
the eastern narthex: and there, above the
great central door into the nave, I saw again
a strange Byzantine bas-relief, that darkly
beautiful fantastic vision of strained figures in
wrinkled wind-blown draperies, Christ giving
to the Apostles the Holy Spirit. And while
I was still wondering at the strange power of
it the huge doors swung slowly back, and I
looked down the endless nave, past round
arch after round arch, to the delicate columns
and Gothic arches of the almost ethereally
spiritual, sunlit choir.

In that moment Vézelay appeared marvel-
lous as ever it was. Then the doors closed
again, and Philippon the incongruously mod-

ern citizen stood beside me chattering of the unequalled length of his nave.

A pardonable incongruity, however, was jolly Philippon : my heart warmed to him now, as standing under the gently terrible Christ, he jested.

" *Hein, monsieur*," said he, taking hold of a rope to ring the great bell. " *Hein, monsieur*, you came to mass this morning, but you aren't a Catholic?"

" No, only a Protestant, why not ?"

Philippon began to ring the bell, and giving me a second rope, he said slyly : —

" Once Henry IV"— clang, broke in the bell, — " asked the Protestants "— clang — " whether he could be saved "— clash — " in the Catholic Church."

Here Philippon left all the work to me, and through the clash and clang of the bell he went on :—

" The Protestants answered ' Yes.' Then Henry asked the Catholic bishops whether he

could be saved in the Protestant church?
'Never,' answered the bishops. Thereupon
the king was a Catholic, and so," added Philippon, with a smile, " so am I."

Could one damn such innocently bargain-
ing, good-natured flippancy? I, for one,
certainly could not; for Philippon, a bit sor-
did but so friendly, was too characteristic of
a modern Vézelay, which was lovable after all.

Its days of enthusiastic faith were long passed.
But kind simplicity had so fully filled its
place that in memory it impresses me even
more than the view through the great doorway, under that strange vision in stone, and
down the long nave. Though this view,
architects tell me, is the most impressive in
any French Romanesque building, and I can
easily believe them, yet I delight still more
in Philippon and in Madame the bakeress
who, as she smiled to me on the village street,
might well have been model for the divine
Mary at Sainte Madelaine. For she and

# Plains and Uplands of Old France

many another peasant are Vézelay. She embodies its true spirit. So does Philippon. And so finally does mine host Gauthillot.

This I know. For after he had strapped up my bundle the morning I left, he brought from the cupboard a bottle of "the queen of all liqueurs," his treasured Chartreuse. And sitting together in his tiled kitchen we drank, he to my journey, and I to France.

Then after much handshaking I started south over the wooded hills.

# Plains and Uplands of Old France

## CHÂTEAU-CHINON

*UP to this highest height o'erlooking height*
  *Rocky defile, and dark, pine-covered knolls,*
 *· To where, translucent blue, the horizon rolls*
*Eternally, here Romans pushed their fight;*
*Here killed and camped; fulfilled their stern de-*
    *light*
    *With measured feast and draughts from copper*
      *bowls;*
    *And, firm to quell and hold rebellious souls,*
*Built, fortified and ruled, with Roman might.*

*No armored conquerors now to savage Franks*
  *Give battle here, and feast. The pillared hall,*
*Now buried deep, rings not with clashing ranks.*
    *But from its cavern-mouth child revels call*
*Down to the deep blue cleft, and from its banks*
*Back to three slender crosses crowning all.*

# Plains and Uplands of Old France

## IN MORVAN

THE clouds which came drifting across the southern hills looked dubious as I began coasting down from Véze-lay; and before I was half way to the valley the faint wind, suddenly strong and cool, brought them black above me. A few large and separate drops fell on the road, the bushes, and the trees. Then faster they fell and thicker till their sound was merged into a sort of seething, and below me, as I hastened on, rain drove across the landscape like a white mist. Under my tires the wet sandy surface of the road hissed like escaping air; and behind I could see a grimey fountain, from my whirling wheel, spurt five feet in air.

Bedraggled then and fearfully bespattered I came into Saint Père-sous-Vézelay and stood in a protected doorway eyeing myself. My feet and legs were encased in sandy mud, and a broad streak of mud, after following my back bone from nether end to neck, mounted to the very top of my cap. Indeed I was an appalling figure, and worse still I was cold. But before I could moan greatly over my plight the sun began to glitter, then shone gay and dazzling on the wet cobble-stones and on the transparent little stream that rushed along the gutter.

So off again among golden wheatfields I followed the valley of the Cure, for a sunlit happy hour, to the bridge of Pierre Perthuis. Its single arch, spanning a cleft, led lightly to an elevation. There, as I sat scraping the mud from shoes and stockings and combing it off my coat, I looked out over a curving pine-clad valley from between whose steep sides the river hastens into the open and under the bridge. Then, mechanically picking sprigs of gorse, I turned from the arch, which all Vézelay recommends to travellers, toward a valley-view which Vézelay modestly forgets; for there, above the silvery Cure the wheatfields and the rolling green hills, Vézelay it-

# Plains and Uplands of Old France

self, shadowy but aspiring, mounts vision-like into the heavens.

But I must be off. Shaking myself till the sunshine to leeward was golden with floating dust, I tossed my sprigs of gorse toward Vézelay in the blue distance; and with this farewell began pedalling up the steadily mounting road.

The climb was disheartening, so nearly desperate indeed that I was soon on the point of dismounting. On the high horizon, however, there appeared a peasant. " If I dismount he will taunt me " thought I, remembering my humiliation in Sainte Colombe, and gallantly I struggled on. But this man, as I met him, called out, "That truly is more laborious than walking."

Such smiling common sense was worse than any taunt: it turned my bravado into abasement and sent me walking slowly on toward Quarré-les-tombes and new surprises. For there again, my preconceptions proved lower,

# Plains and Uplands of Old France

and also higher, than the fact. The thousand tombs miraculously prepared for Gerard's dead warriors turned out to be a dozen or so great oblong stones with rounded edges. But the natives of this upland village showed themselves drolly civilized. Indeed the conversation of one, whom I overheard as I sipped my *grenadine* in the little café, smacked of the École des Beaux Arts. "The view from this window," he said to his companion, a workman in a faded blouse, "the view from this window is not beautiful. It has striking features, I admit. But for a scene to be beautiful some arrangement, some harmony is needful." And in the æsthetic discussion which followed, the man in a faded blouse gradually revealed himself as a traveller, so cultivated and amiable a traveller, in fact, that over his absinthe he was soon talking with me about the picturesqueness of the river Tarn.

Here, surely, was an unexpected acquaintance: all Burgundy could hardly show me

# Plains and Uplands of Old France

such another. So I thought as I made my
way from Quarré-les-tombes along the "forest
road." And I was right. But Morvan, as
they call the Burgundian upland which now
surrounded me, Morvan was prompt with a
new surprise. By this narrow and stony road
it was already welcoming me into almost New
England woods. Above me the trees of my
home whispered well-known rustling secrets
to the broken sunshine; on the right, where
the hillside fell steep toward leafy depths,
familiar waters glistened; and before me the
road, turning a little, led intimately down,
down toward what I almost believed the New
Hampshire lake of my earliest summers.

The brightness among the trees narrowed,
however, as I came near. I saw the Cure again,
hastening musically over its rocks toward a
dark ravine. And Morvan, the same wilful
Morvan that had drenched me with its rain,
encased me in its mud, and sent a saddening
peasant to me from his hilltop, now lured me

through alders to the singing solitude of the river. So resting soon in silvery waves which laughed across my shoulders, I floated down stream, and as I floated gazed aloft past yellow *fleurs de lys* and past the metallic-green dragon-flies that darted hither and thither across the blue of an infinitely ethereal sky.

Could any region be long so caressing, I wondered; for after giving such delights, it seemed to me, even Morvan must soon turn harsh. Yet as I wandered beyond the river I found for a time only smiling hills, low and undulating like land-locked waves; and when in the afternoon I came at last among darker, more tumultuous hills, sunlight and golden stretches of furze brightened their bleakness; forget-me-nots, with white orchids and purple, raised their blossoms delicately along the steep roadside; and banks of wild thyme offered balmy resting places. So continually refreshed I climbed and coasted, climbed again and raced between sparkling gutters till in the midst of

# Plains and Uplands of Old France

more wooded highlands I reached, toward evening, a great hill. And just below its peak I found at last Château-Chinon, the capital of Morvan.

Disdaining the ease of valleys it stood facing the brisk wind some eighteen hundred feet above the sea. As I climbed past its low white houses it seemed bleak, almost deserted. Only here and there a lamplit window shone yellow in the dusk. But beyond the little town, a red and golden sunset called me to the peak where once a Gallic town had stood, then a Roman camp. Seating myself there above the cave-like vaults of a later castle, I watched the darkening cleft and the stormy hills that rolled endlessly about me. And as darkness sank over them I slept, leaning against one of three tall crosses that stand there dominating all Morvan.

# Plains and Uplands of Old France

## PÉRIGUEUX

*DOME upon dome, high in the firmament*
*And vision-deep within the river's trance,*
*A phantom mosque from the far Orient*
*Floats silver-clad among the stars of France.*
*Hither from realms of war and winding dance*
*Wafted on smouldering breezes indolent,*
*It rests beneath the western angels' glance,*
*Reborn in snowy stone magnificent.*

*No Moslem kneels below the choir dome*
*But wingèd voices, frail as ocean foam,*
*Rise toward our starry Lady of the Sea;*
*And through the sanctuary's wonder-night,*
*Radiantly pale one hallowed eastern light*
*Worships the Lord in trembling mystery.*

# Plains and Uplands of Old France

## WHERE THE ENGLISH RULED

ROM the market-place of Péri-
gueux where dark women, their
heads wound about with red or
yellow, bargain beneath the tower
of Saint Front, I followed white roads ever
eastward. Domes, and tower too, dropped behind a slope, rose and sank again. And the
little river Vézère led me south between gray
cliffs, sometimes pierced with the windows of
dizzy rock-hewn homes, again bearing in a recess above the poplar-tops some castle whence
robbers, long ago, swooped upon the traveller.
Grateful for the safety of these democratic
days I rested in the shade of bright-leaved but-
ternut-trees, and made my way onward, lazy
but self-dependent, till sunset glowed around
me. Then urged by a wish to sleep that night
in the forgotten democratic town of Montpazier, I sacrificed roadside pleasure to the speed
of a joggling third-class railway-carriage.

# Plains and Uplands of Old France

As I got in an amiable peasant-woman moved her basket with its quacking imprisoned goose, and motioned me to sit in its place.

"That is restful after bicycling? *Hein?*" she queried. And on my thanking her for my cushionless comfort she fell into chat. A hog of I dare not say how many kilos had been sold that day. Ah, his fatness was a marvel, so wonderful indeed, that while the tremulous lamp began to grow bright in the increasing darkness, a toothless peasant opposite me lisped out commendations. He had seen but one greater hog, and that, he informed us, was his grandfather's. Then, withdrawing his feet from straw-stuffed wooden shoes, he rested silently. But his smooth and alert, almost boyish face remained keen for each pointed word till, at the solitary little station of Le Got, he and I stepped out.

"You have stabled your horse in the baggage van?" he joked as I lifted down my

# Plains and Uplands of Old France

bicycle; and he chuckled to himself so gaily, as he trudged off, that I hated to leave him.

But hurrying forward in the cold starlit air I came over low hills, to a slight valley and up a curving slope to a gate-tower at the middle of a high long wall.

"République Française" was printed in great letters on a strip of white, dimly visible over the pointed archway; for though built by the second King Henry of England this walled town, Montpazier, was now as French as the once English region all around. Every mark, indeed, of the old English days seemed lost. Modern life had left no gate in the gateway, and in the broad smooth grooves no sliding portcullis. Darkness made the straight street blank except where the lamp of an industrious carpenter cast a square of light on the rough ground. And silence winged its way tremulous before me till under the dusky mass of the church I heard a sharp scratch and saw the blue flame of a match.

# Plains and Uplands of Old France

Where might I lodge, I asked the man revealed by the tiny growing light. Then following the roadway under broad arches that support the projecting second-stories of houses about the square I came to a side street, down which was an inn; and seated at a bare table, there, under a swinging lamp, I drank to the independence of the great democracy.

"Ah, it is a fête-day in your country?" asked the old-maidish daughter of the house.

"Yes, the Fourth of July," said I, and explained the glory of it.

"Indeed? But tell me, are they still at war in your country?" she asked.

Cuba being at the time but a faint cloud, I laughed as I told her that the Civil War was a thing of history and the Revolution dimly pre-historic. Then following the strong, turbaned mother I climbed to an upper room where dreams were lurking, dreams of this mediæval commune and its equal citizens devoted peacefully by faith to church and lord.

44

# Plains and Uplands of Old France

At dawn, moreover, I found actual Montpazier still quaint with a tinge of its primitive
aspect. The town-plan remained clear and
rigid, and three of the six ancient gate-towers
still rose above the walls. On the carpenter's
street of the night before I discovered, besides
the church, an ancient dark stone house with
round arches. Again in the central square
Galmot the blacksmith had a Renaissance
abode. At the opposite corner, too, the town
well-house, a little stone affair with a window
in one wall, stood firm; and to this immemo-
rial centre of gossip and good-fellowship, the
citizens, men and women, still brought their
great water-cans, and chatting together let them
easily down, and hoisted them with fine swinging movements of the whole body.

How differently democratic, how subtly
subservient, and yet how free these people
might have become, under English rule. So
I reflected as I lingered in the square. But

the sun was getting well above the roofs. I turned away; and after a breakfast of bread and goat's milk coffee at the inn, set out from its vine-shaded doorway.

From the town gate a glaring white road led me far along a tongue of high land. Behind me the towers and walls of little Montpazier disappeared below green vineyards. Forward on each side stretched slight valleys, their chalky slopes showing whitish through the vegetation, as plaster shows through the color of wasting frescoes. And the sun overhead shone upon the slopes, and glared so dazzlingly from the white road, that all the landscape was dark by contrast, so dark indeed, that when the castle-like towers of Beaumont church first appeared before me, they seemed like the sharp reflections in a curved black mirror.

A lizard shot across the road; a peasant, his boots spattered with blue phylloxera-medicine, and a can of the same on his back,

# Plains and Uplands of Old France

gave me greeting as he entered his vineyard;
and I whirred down into Beaumont.

The square of that once English village
should have been like the Montpazier square,
surrounded by a roadway under the arched sup-
ports of overhanging houses. But only a few
arches showed the ancient plan; and never, it
seemed, had a town well gathered the citizens
together in common work. Hardly a peasant was to be seen. As I glanced up at the
church, its warlike towers, one partly ruined,
the other still strongly machicolated, reminded
me incongruously that the day was sacred. I
came closer to the church door. A great sun-
dial on the nearer tower's flank cast a shrunken
shadow near the figure XII. And through
the almost windowless, bush-grown walls came
a sound of general singing.

Within, I found all Beaumont. On the
right sat the men, on the left the women,
many in light blue, and more with a dull yel-

47

low handkerchief wound skilfully about the hair and falling in a single fold between the shoulders. Those touches of yellow were exquisite notes in the church dimness; and a young man, now and then, seemed aware of their charm — or of charms more personal.

Gradually, however, while all knelt, the straying glances of both men and girls centered on a tiny dog who had approached from nowhere and now stood perkily in the centre of the aisle. Putting his head on one side he looked toward the altar and toward the back of the somewhat nearer beadle. That functionary, superb in a plumed and silvery cocked hat, moved his foot a little and shifted his grasp on the official halberd. Evidently he felt the minute eye fixed on his back, for he fidgeted and turned. The dog took to almost vibratory ear-scratching. The beadle, scenting irreverence, frowned, and after some mediation marched on him, halberd pompously in hand. Then the dog cocked one soft ear into questioning stiffness, hesitated a moment, and scampered between the official legs straight for the altar.

The second bell was ringing for the elevation of the host. Throughout the congregation decorous awe contended with smiles. The beadle was stern. Desperately dignified he countermarched upon the dog. But the microscopic culprit, venturesome even now, dashed back past the halberd. Then, while the bell rang a third time, he skedaddled to the entrance steps, and there sat wagging his tail against the dusty stone at my feet.

"Under England and the English church, would this life have been so full of color?" I wondered, as, standing in the doorway, I watched the smiling company scatter after mass. Hardly. But England was well forgotten. "People *say* that the English formerly possessed this region," said a sceptical gray-beard during our midday meal.

# Plains and Uplands of Old France

And over the coffee mine host discoursed on national calamities which, as I thought, would never have occurred if the spirit of England had been remembered and followed.

" We must fight," said mine host. " Yes, by keeping Alsace-Lorraine, Bismarck has roused our pride. Otherwise we should thank him for having rid us of that cursed Badinguet."

" Badinguet ? "

" Ah ! Do you know the story ? Napoleon killed a man named Badinguet, in Strasbourg. So here we always call him Badinguet." And when I left, he was calling "Badinguet" the curse of France.

To me, however, the curse of France seemed a national childishness so like mine host's that on my way across the valley, I wasted possibly humorous moments on pity. But part way up the opposite slope, I met a peasant with a gleam in his eye, who looked most invitingly like my old friend of the night be-

# Plains and Uplands of Old France

fore. So I stopped and we fell a-chatting on our remoteness from cities.

"Yet, in these days we are near to Paris after all," said he, pointing to the telegraph-wire strung high above the roadside.

"Yes, that brings news quickly," I answered.

"Ah, quickly indeed," said he.

"Well, how quickly?"

He considered a moment. Then, with a smile, "See," he explained, "the telegraph is like an enormous dog. His tail is in Paris, and his head, here. At Paris they press on the end of his tail, so. And in his head, here, he knows it — *at once*. That is the telegraph. *Hein?*"

So I went on toward Saint Avit-le-Sénieur and Cadoin and the Dordogne, hopeful again for France. For were not citizens of such humor the salvation of our own Democracy?

51

# Plains and Uplands of Old France

## THE MIRACLE OF OUR LADY'S BELL

*HERE, Lady, to thy rock-girt shrine*
*Where hangs the iron bell,*
*We come to greet thy grace divine,*
*And sing through all the dell.*
 *Thou savest thy sailors, friend of the poor,*
 *Beloved sweet Lady of Roc-Amadour.*

*For while a grim, dark hurricane*
*Once lashed the northern sea,*
*We Bretons in our fear and pain*
*Cried fervently to thee.*

*And here within thy distant shrine*
*The ancient iron bell,*
*Which tolls not but by grace divine,*
*Tolled out a miracle.*

*So from the lashing hurricane*
*And from the grim north sea,*
*We who were saved are come again,*
*And sing with love to thee.*
 *Thou savest thy sailors, friend of the poor,*
 *Beloved sweet Lady of Roc-Amadour.*

# Plains and Uplands of Old France
## THE DESERT AND A SHRINE

### I.

NTO a passable-looking hotel in Souillac I wandered one evening, weary from a day of dust, and there, besides fair cleanliness and rest, found the surprising stimulus of exotic art. On those obscure walls, lost in a dead town, hung fine Chinese swords, spears, and grotesque masks; and on the inlaid sideboard in the dining-room stood pieces of Chinese porcelain and piles of beautiful Chinese plates. Here, in short, were rarities enough to make one's eyes stare. But as I asked mine host next day, how did they come here ?

" My son,— " he gruffly answered.

" Ah, he was in China ? In commerce ? Or as a soldier ? "

" Soldier — "

" In Tonquin ? "

# Plains and Uplands of Old France

" Seven years — "

Then with head hanging low, and knees apart, the father sat taciturn ; and in his silence there was more tragedy, more poignant mourning, than in endless lamenting words.

So it was with a mind dulled by sadness that I went down to the domed abbey church, Not essentially unlike many another of this region it seemed, as I glanced at its walls ; but as soon as I had passed through the low side-door, the central pillar of the great eastern portal startled me.

The wild, strangely fantastic sculptures, crawling criss-cross upward between its scalloped sides, seemed to writhe in the darkness. Slimy biting things, at the base, almost wriggled toward the rent and rending birds that struggled in and out through the fierce medley, up, up to where man at last, himself wounded, struggled among the highest.  Squirming and ferocious, their battle seemed like the fury of beasts petrified a million years since in some

# Plains and Uplands of Old France

marsh-invaded jungle. Or was it the raging of heathen gods? A Hindoo hell? Some such guess, I vaguely remembered, had been made by learned men. But as I stood gazing at this pillar, the power of its animals and the bent weakness of man at their head seemed at last, what perhaps it is, the stony fantasy in which some sculptor of the dark ages hewed out his prophetic nightmare of our modern Darwinism.

My notion was retrograde; I pushed it away. But the pillar itself, no matter how conceived, remained so darkly foreign, so persistently disquieting, that I was glad, on leaving it, to look forward toward green fields. After less than an hour among them, however, the chalky road led me under blue-gray cliffs to the Dordogne, and abruptly dived into its waters.

" Sacred thousand names of a name ! " as a French companion of mine had exclaimed on my leaving him, recently, with his bicycle tire collapsed; "Sacred thousand names of a name!" I muttered. But a fisherman on the opposite bank soon came over in his black scow and ferried me across, man and bicycle. Lucky fisherman! he loved his surroundings even better that the *sous* that he earned; he loved the swift, dark water, the caves, the cliffs, and the gray hill-sides so steep that the loose stones are always ready to slide into the stream; and he loved the chestnut trees on the dazzling green plain where we landed. All day he fished there happily. But I labored up hill from the plain, then down the steep to where the Dordogne drinks in the Ouysse. With a boat I might have followed the little river to its very source, two huge springs near Roc-Amadour, my destination. With my bicycle, however, I climbed a road of split stones up from the green fields and further and further from the loud metallic buzzing of locusts, till I came at last to a desert plain, the Causse de Gramat; there I

# Plains and Uplands of Old France

rode on wild thyme, and on grass munched short by sheep. Again I walked along cart-tracks and over desolate stretches of loose gray stones that reflect the scorching heat of the sun. And though the air was so dry that I could see the distant hillsides of the Dordogne as clear and sharp as if through a telescope, still sweat continually trickled into my eyes.

But even in this desert, more exotic than China and fiercer in its heat than the ferocious carving at Souillac, even here there were de-lights for the wanderer. Under some oaks I found a muddy pool in which bullet-shaped tadpoles with thready tails rose for the whiffs of air, and dropped again to the bottom. Who could resist their example?—Then muddy and cool, and gleefully munching a dry crust, I led my bicycle down a rocky water-way to cultivated fields and a peasant's house.

Just inside the low doorway a brown woman,

# Plains and Uplands of Old France

with a neat little beard and a black straw hat, returned my greeting and responded to my tale of famine. She would do her best, she said. And while I rested beside the cat on a bench she busily disappeared. With side glances at the cauldron over the blazing brush fire, I cut myself a slice of the gray bread on the table before me. As I chewed I admired the primitive brass saucer-lamp that hung from a smoky beam, the big fire-dogs, and the neat ranges of plates on black shelves with spoons hanging in order below. I studied the tall clock, ticking between the bed and the deep-arched recess where water is to be found. "Must I slake my own thirst?" I wondered. But just then the brown woman came back with a great saucer of foaming milk. And after straining it through a clean, coarse cloth she set it before me with a Roc-Amadour cheese and some odd, nutty wine which jovially capped my long and vivifying feast.

"What do I owe?" I asked finally.

# Plains and Uplands of Old France

" Nothing, if you choose."

" But, *madame* — ! "

" I leave it to you, sir. Surely you know."

" *Madame*, I have not the vaguest shadow of an idea. I confide myself to you. I put myself entirely in your hands."

So I got a conscientious reckoning : one cent for the cheese, perhaps a cent for the bread, a cent for the milk — as for the wine, she hardly knew — perhaps five cents for everything. I paid ten ; and we parted with friendly handshakings and a hearty "*au revoir.*"

Off again I started for a second half-day's ride, by vague stony tracks, across the desert. But even before my bearded peasant-woman's house was entirely hidden by a lonely clump of trees, I came upon a highway and suddenly looked into a cleft-like valley along whose nearer side the brown-roofed houses and the great gray monastery of Roc-Amadour clam-

59

bered almost to my feet. So unexpected was the sight—a village revealed in the depths where a plain had seemed to stretch desolately forever — so unexpected was this that I almost laughed; and I rejoiced in the picturesqueness of it, and wondered, as the road turned away, how I might ever reach it. Abruptly, however, the road turned again, this time into a tunnel, from which in an instant it emerged and brought me sunnily down to a village street and the demure little doorway of the Golden Lion.

Within I found simplicity almost as rustic as in the peasant-house above. As I sat in my room under the roof and looked across the narrow valley to the gray and white crags that rose into a solid almost eastern sky, I heard the incessant vibratory grating of locusts and now and then the jangling bells of a donkey-cart. But the charm of the Golden Lion was not a matter of such simple country alone: it was a subtler thing, a floating impression of

# Plains and Uplands of Old France

pilgrim's prayers, and still more a *naïveté* of spirit pervasive in the whole house, but centered, perhaps, in "*mademoiselle.*" For when she had brought my larks and truffles to the pilgrim's dining hall, her face was bright with the unquestioning faith of ages gone, and she told me artlessly, and as a matter of mere fact, how the iron bell in the chapel often miraculously rang when Our Lady, the "star of the sea," heard the supplication of the faithful sailors.

"After it has rung," she said, "Breton fishermen come to thank our Lady of Roc-Amadour; for it is she who has saved them from the hurricane."

Her quaint story, even more seductive than truffles, brought me eagerly on my way toward the desert shrine. I hurried down through the doorway; pushed past a donkey whose switching tail and top-heavy load of hay barred the street from side to side; and striding on between low houses and beneath the over-

61

# Plains and Uplands of Old France

powering sheer height of the monastery wall,
I soon reached the sacred steps, a hundred or
more, that lead tirelessly up and up to a little
courtyard sweet with the perfume of incense.
There on a stone bench I rested dreamily
and long, looking from wall to rock-wall and
up to the cliff which darkens Roc-Amadour,
this home of Saint Amadour, the Rock-Lover.
Then after a glance at the Byzantine frescoes,
faintly harmonious on the bleak gray walls, I
passed through an arched doorway and stood
in the Virgin's chapel, a holy of holies so
calm in its darkness that I wondered how I
dared enter.

Against a smoky wall of rock, candles flared
before hanging manacles and crutches; and
opposite, somewhere in the night, tiny flames
flickered beneath flags which drooped, vague
and dim, from the invisible vaulting. There
was no other light. I almost felt my way
forward, past kneeling sisters in black, till
I could see the Byzantine lamps in which lived

# Plains and Uplands of Old France

the endlessly flickering flames. Then at last before the altar, I looked up beyond rich, dull metal work to the black virgin enthroned on high, robed in white and forever venerable.

Gradually, however, as I stood where Saint Veronica, Saint Martial and Roland the hero had knelt, the darkness grew less dense ; and while I still thought of Roland thrusting his sword in the rock before going hence to Roncevaux, I began to notice the offerings of modern warriors. In a glazed frame I spied a pair of gold-thread epaulettes, and around them five medals, on one of which I made out the inscription " Meuriche, chef de bataillon, 91$^{me}$ de ligne, 1855." Nearer the door I found two military crosses, signs of devotion to the " Honor and Fatherland " ; then a medal of the Italian campaign, another for Algerian service, another stamped " Sevastapool." And at last, close to the miraculous bell, I looked up and saw hanging from the vault, a miniature ship.

# Plains and Uplands of Old France

That offering from childlike grateful Brit-
tany bore my memories of the Causse and
fantastic Souillac towards lands of soft forget-
fulness ; and the Breton spirit sang around
me as I lingered near the miraculous bell.
But when at dusk I came through the black-
ness of a vaulted passage and out on a high
pathway, the desert above seemed to throb
with haunting desolation. The voice of the
village idiot rang out beneath the stars and
rattled among the cold, almost phosphorescent
cliffs. Its wildness was like that rockstrewn
plain, bleak in the night. But now before
me, I saw welcoming lights in the Golden
Lion where Bretons lodge ; and soon seated
there with the fond believing hostess, I heard
again how Our Lady of Roc-Amadour rescues
her Bretons from the North sea's fury.

# Plains and Uplands of Old France

## THE BROOKS

*BENEATH a sun-lit chestnut-tree*
*Whose leaves like emeralds hang*
*A ripple-sprite in agony*
*Thus madly sang : —*
    *I'm gay, I'm gay as the light of day,*
    *My laugh has the cricket's cheer,*
    *For I toss on my world-old bed of gold,*
    *And I wait for my lover dear.*

*Beneath the dark entombing stones*
*Through fissures black and long*
*Her lover sang in echoing tones*
*A steady song : —*
    *I fight, I fight through eternal light,*
    *I shout with warrior-cheer,*
    *And my life is strong with conquering*
        *strife*
    *As I fight toward my mistress dear,*

*Then leaped the buried brook to light,*
*And swift in revelry*
*His waters sped with the ripple-sprite*
*Toward life in the deathless sea.*

# Plains and Uplands of Old France

## FANTASTIC FRIENDS IN A
## FANTASTIC LAND

HILE a steady procession of two-wheeled ox-carts came at dusk into Gramat, I sat watching the great oxen. With patient brows they pushed against the padded cross-bars that stretched, on each side of the poles, out to their bound horns; and through double veils of cord, one short, one long and tasselled at the nose, they looked ever forward with soft, weary eyes.

They had come with trailing loads of hay from a region rich in crops; and they were bound for the desert. So much I gleaned from a chaos of *patois* as the drivers stopped a moment for their " little glass"; then I unregretfully watched them pass on into evening quiet; for my host seemed willing, and my chunky hostess seemed eager, to follow up previous talks.

# Plains and Uplands of Old France

"After all," said the good-naturedly sceptical woman, "After all, to be honest like
those fellows — some of 'em — that's the im-
portant point. As for going to mass or the
Protestant church, it's all one to me. I don't
care a fig. But the neighbors ——!" She
raised most eloquent hands heavenward.

"Well, the neighbors?" I queried.

"They think of nothing else. Listen —
in a commune over there"— pointing toward
the *causse* — "in a commune over there a band
of ladies got tired of their priest and built a
Protestant temple. Then were they satisfied?
Not at all. When they found that they could
have no broom-sprinklings at their christen-
ings and their marriages and their funerals,
they were *frightened*— yes. And now the
temple is closed."

Here an urchin trudging along the road,
interrupted with a whine for bread or a *sou*.

"But I gave to your mother this morning,"
said madame.

# Plains and Uplands of Old France

" My mother is dead.  I live all alone with my father —" the boy mock-piteously pled.

In the dusk mine host leaned forward till lamplight from the door gleamed on his white moustache.  "And your mother," he suggested, "your mother died a year before you were born ?"

The boy grinned slily.  "My *father* was curé at Limoges," said he, and went his way.

"Good-for-nothing rascal !" laughed madame.

" No madame, not good-for-nothing.  He makes your country life less dull."

Ah, it was dull, she answered.  But then, since her husband's health required it, they must be content to live here.  Yes, her husband's health had made it necessary to give up Parisian life and their little laundry near Notre Dame.  And here they were.

Ah, here they were, the husband broke in with a violence oddly contradicted by the softness of his deep voice.  Here they were, only too willing to work, yet hardly able to subsist, because whatever they attempted, taxes and monopoly chained them. He owned good soil for tobacco ; and monopoly forbade his cultivating it. He bought good wines to sell ; and taxes, first on the right to sell, then on every barrel brought into his cellar, made profit honestly impossible. All this to support a corrupt government in a mad policy of colonization and revenge ! Why fight in China and plot invasions of Germany when injustice reigned at home ? The government was mad. "There must be a revolution," said this Parisian socialist. " I tell you everything must be completely changed. I have one son in the army and another studying on a government purse. So I am benefited as well as oppressed. Yet, I insist that the revolution must come."

The phrase rang in my mind ; and I was still assaulted by echoes of its modern

half-justified spirit of unrest when I came,
next day, past springs to a stream that van-
ishes disconcertingly in the earth.   But its
discontent died away as I listened to the dual
sound of a subterranean brook and a sunlit
hurrying rill ; and free in spirit I passed from
their harmony on to a pungent discord no
less characteristic of the Midi.   The chim-
neys of blighting iron-works, veritable hell-
mouths, rose near me.   And through the
midst of them, forward again next day, I
pushed into a wooded valley which led upward till there appeared above smutty village
houses, a red gap in a sunlit hill with white
and bluish smoke rising persistently against the
whitish-blue sky.

The sight was enough to lure me up half a
mile, through hot sun and fresh breeze, to a
high-perched house and a wheat-patch, and
from there along a desolate ridge of crumb-
ling, red earth into smoke.   Pushing my way
windward, I came through to air again, and

# Plains and Uplands of Old France

looked down into the gap. Its sides, here red, there white, there oozy with yellow and streaked with gray, were rotten and ready to fall. At the bottom the sunlight trembled through hot air, and up from the lowest helter-skelter confusion of rocks, smoke rose steadily. Again from a stretch of powdery ground, to which I came over crackled red clay, tiny whiffs of smoke puffed into the sulphurous air. Near it, however, a crater of spongy rocks, was cold. Cold, too, seemed the circle of jerky, round-topped hills that grimly hem in the north. But eastward there was smoke again, lingering in clouds beside feverishly green woods. Everywhere, indeed, the hills showed lively warmth or the yellow blight of intense heat, the smoke of underground fire, or the desolation of dead flames. Everywhere the fire was dying, raging, or kindling in the earth. For, says tradition, the English, when driven from France, revengefully kindled a coal vein here. In fact, eras be-

71

fore the English even began to exist, fires had kindled themselves, and were spreading in the sulphur and coal of the Cransac hills.

The weird, half-volcanic effects of the hidden fire kept me long spying about the height. At last, however, tired of strangeness I trotted down the dead-yellow slopes. Passing a statuesque girl, on whose head a copper water-vase glistened in the afternoon sun, I came to the village. Between smudgy, flat-faced houses, I walked down the dusty street, and at a corner met a group of miners, each with a bottle in a straw basket slung from his shoulder. They have thirsty work, poor fellows : they must dig and pick their coal in a race with fire, and sometimes heat drives them from a gallery still rich in coal. No wonder, then, that they are dreary, perhaps angry like mine host at Gramat ; and no wonder that I gladly left watching them to enter even a wretched inn. There I supped wretchedly. But thence again, in the deepening twilight,

# Plains and Uplands of Old France

I escaped and followed the valley upward toward a happier region.

It grew velvety dark. Behind me, between black hills and the nocturnal blue sky, a light from subterranean flames glowed distant and more distant. It sank behind a turbulent horizon. The hours of earliest night passed silent and swift; and I came into the village of Marcillac where all things slept.

There was no lamp in the Traveller's Hotel, and in the neighboring houses not a candle. But down the hushed street shone the oblong light of an open door; and over it, as I came near, I spied that hospitable symbol, an unwithered bush. Freely, then, I entered; and in the kitchen greeted my hostess, a smiling but sadly hunchbacked girl.

Yes, certainly I might spend the night, she assured me; and taking with her a candle, she went to prepare my room.

Sitting by the open fire I began to examine

the crane. But now a nasal voice greeted me. I looked up; and beyond a jockey-like being in the dining-room doorway, I saw, bright in the lamp-light beyond him, the necklace and white breast of a woman in black, *décolletée*.

"*Monsieur* is a traveller?" asked the man, ignoring the question in my look. "And has he come from far?" he persisted. "Ah, indeed! From America!" With that the dapper little fellow, checkered waistcoat and all, came suddenly near, and with head tipping from side to side and shoulders lurching, he rattled on: He himself, had once almost gone to Vash-angton — to New Yorrke — to Chicago — to Boston — in fact to all the great cities of America! Yes, Madame Sarah Bernhardt — did I know that great tragédienne? — Madame Sarah Bernhardt had done her very best to persuade him. But he could not make up his mind to it; no, not even for her sake! For there was *one* thing that he feared, but *one* thing — the sea! Ah, he knew the sea, he

# Plains and Uplands of Old France

knew the sea! Thirty-six hours he had been tossed by a terrific storm — on his way to Tunis.

He paused.

"Tunis?" I inquired.

"Yes, Tunis! I have been there," said he, "yes, I have seen service. Otherwise this ——" And fingering a dirty bluish ribbon in his button-hole he silently, expressively shook his head.

Meantime his companion had come to the door. Leaning languidly against it, she listened with an air of submission that made me scrutinize her. What was she, I wondered. But now the pretty hunchbacked girl came to show me my room.

"They are artists!" She said with awe, as we climbed toward the attic.

"Ah! that explains the lady's dress," I suggested.

Yes, the dress would naturally surprise me: it was unusual in the country, she gently explained. "But, in the great cities ——!!"

# Plains and Uplands of Old France

Her gesture was an oration. It expressed all that she could imagine of the splendor of balls and rich levees, this and her mute thankfulness that celebrities familiar with these things were actually present, lodging in her inn.

"They are *artists!*" was all she could say, as she left my room.

In that belief I slept, but next morning, near the village of Saint Cyprien, I met these "artists," vagabond performers in a vagabond carriage, he, self-contented and talkative as ever, but she, poor little woman, sadly conscious of the sham that he was. She looked down as we exchanged greetings. Then their road branched from mine. And as they trotted off, this grotesque pathetic pair became for me odd reminders of the two streams that I had seen, uniting on the desert's edge, and flowing, they knew not whither.

# Plains and Uplands of Old France

## JOCUS SANCTAE FIDIS

*SINCE Jesus, who for sinners bled,*
*Upon an ass from Egypt fled*
*Sainte Foy hath alway given ear*
    *Where men have prayed,*
    *Or asses brayed,*
*To her in pious fear.*

*With faith, then, once to her abode*
*A pilgrim came who on the road*
*Had left his lazy ass for dead;*
    *And, "Saving Maid,"*
    *The pilgrim prayed,*
*"Raise him from Death's cold bed."*

*And lest mere prayer should not suffice*
*He offered gifts. Then in a trice*
*Sainte Foy appeared, armed with a goad.*
    *And sore dismayed*
    *The dead ass brayed*
*While cattle loudly lowed.*

*In witness of which miracle*
*The pilgrim left his ass to dwell*
*Among her gifts, a gift of price.*
    *And to this day*
    *The ass doth bray*
*To her in paradise.*

# Plains and Uplands of Old France

## CONQUES

**F**OLLOWING the red little river Dourdou, as it flowed murmuring past a mill, I entered a wooded gap. Steep chestnut slopes on the right, and on the left, craggy black hills rose some four hundred feet toward a narrowing band of sky. Through overhanging trees the sunlight shone on the road in blotches that danced and glared, then dazzled the faces of peasants who came toward me, urging their pigs and more tractable sheep toward Saint Cyprien and the fair. "Yes," said one lanky fellow whom I greeted as I passed. "Yes, it was hot, indeed," and on he passed toward the unshaded open. But as I went on, I found leafy shelter, water trickling here and there from mossy rocks, and at last, toward noon, a refreshing promise — the high-perched village of Conques, and rising from among its roofs, the three bluntly pointed towers of Sainte Foy.

# Plains and Uplands of Old France

" Good day, sir," I heard, as after climbing
by a zig-zag road, I came toward the church;
and a bearded dwarf, not more than three feet
high, stood before me clutching his black
blouse in one hand, and with the other baring
his head as he bowed from the hips and sim-
pered. I passed on. But still bowing he
followed; and with grotesquely unconscious
appropriateness, he made himself my guide to
the strangest wild work done in honor of
Sainte Foy.

This great bas-relief, as I first looked up
over the western door, seemed soft with a certain aspect of tenderness; its time-worn col-
oring, its dull yellows, reds and greens formed
such a gentle harmony as one finds in some
rare tapestries. But here was depicted a dream
whose fascination was too high and too grotesque for any tapestry. Fateful and inexor-
able, Christ forever reigns over this Hell and
Heaven of stone. On His right the saved
stand in blessed dignity : on His left the

damned writhe in chaos. And below Him
all flesh rises to be judged in that final judgment from the immediate terror of which man
had not long escaped when some dramatic
sculptor imagined here its horrors and felici-
ties. He saw and carved the gate of Heaven
shut against all but the elect whom an angel
receives after their weighing. But for all
those weighed and found wanting he left the
gate of Hell standing open, and the great
dragon-mouth of Hell agape. Into it a bent
Simian devil throws the damned. They are
gulped down and drawn headlong into the
depths of Hell. And there a knight in full
armor is tortured ; a man and a woman con-
demned for adultery are hanged by one cord ;
a devil tears out a slanderer's tongue ; a hog
and a rabbit roast a gormand ; and in the
midst of all, Beelzebub, his feet resting on a
sloth, listens to the secret whisperings of one
of his angels, and grinning, shows ghastly
teeth.

# Plains and Uplands of Old France

"The dark ages!" I involuntarily exclaimed. The dwarf, however, who still stood beside me, merely smiled and pointed to inscriptions cut into the stone.

"Sinners," read the mediæval Latin, "if ye do not mend your ways, know that ye must suffer a terrible judgment. The wicked are tormented with pains and burned with fire; and in the midst of demons they must tremble and groan perpetually." But—"For the glory of Heaven are given to the elect glory, peace, rest and light without end."

So much I read to the dwarf, who bowed as I gave him a copper or two. Then, though he was still bobbing politely up and down, I entered the church.

There, it seemed to me, a calm certainty of spirit must always have given peace to men. For the plain round arches of the lower story and of the high triforium gallery gained a great impressiveness from the simplicity of the dark vaulting. No criss-cross of groins, but

# Plains and Uplands of Old France

according to the custom of southern France, a barrel-vault like the roof of a tunnel, covered the nave. And in its heights, not even contrasts of light and shade disturbed the mind. Above the hidden windows of the gallery the outer glare could find no place to enter ; and the ancient solemnity would almost have been gloom, had it not been for the pretty tower over the crossing of nave and transepts. Through the windows of its eight sides the sun shone brilliantly, lit the blue Byzantine angels supporting alternate walls ; lit the yellowish pillars below, and glowed even to the altar. So the grave church had a happy aspect. Moreover bits of carving, remnants of fresco and the twelfth century wrought-iron screens about the choir so tempered its great simplicity with richness that it was beautiful.

Such at least was my rather vague impression as I glanced about me in the coolness. But when, perchance, I looked out through the south door, the church seemed by magic to gain individuality. At once it connected itself with the opposite hill and polished black slate shimmering through the hot air, with the white-blossomed chestnuts, with all the life of the unspoiled highlands, and especially with a gentle little man whose bald pate shone in the sunshine as he gathered lilies in the church garden.

"You know Sainte Foy?" he asked as he came in. And after he had placed his flowers on the altar, "You must see her abbey," he went on in his rather Spanish French, and off we started among what is left of the old buildings. Suddenly, however, he stopped, picked up a great iron collar, clasped it about his neck, and looking proudly up at me said, "I have seen many a collar like that clasped but not unclasped — Sainte Foy released a prisoner from this. The iron-work in her church was made from chains that she had broken. But now she leaves fifty negroes at a time chained together by their necks."

# Plains and Uplands of Old France

Yes, he had seen it all in Africa, where he had worked for the faith. But now, as he meekly said, he was permitted to rest here; and, for the faith, he did his best to serve "Monsieur le Curé." Even now he must be off; he must pick more flowers in the garden.

But before we parted, the devout Spaniard sold me a little life of Sainte Foy, sweet with his own childlike spirit. Through the rough hours of an upland thunder-storm, it sang to me quaintly of a twice-martyred child, of her strong life on earth, and her childlike immortality. The Romans, it seemed, had burned and beheaded her when she was only twelve; and in heaven, she had scarcely grown older. With the tenderest naïveté she had given not only eyes to the eyeless and twins to the barren, but life to the dead. One favored ass, whom she found dead on the road, had already been partly skinned. Yet while the owner was praying for him, she sent him to Conques

# Plains and Uplands of Old France

at a brisk gallop, braying thankfully, for his wounds were perfectly healed.

The fame of Sainte Foy spread, accordingly, to Germany and Spain and even, at last, to her American city of Santa Fé. But she was always most intimately known among the people of southern France. To them she appeared during the middle ages, in continual visions, asking — celestial child that she was — for presents of jewelry. When these were promptly given she rewarded the givers : when they were refused she meted out miraculous punishment. So her miracles became a bye-word. In the church at Conques, peasants sang cheerily of " Sainte Foy's jokes." And though the monks were displeased and reproved the singers and locked them out, Sainte Foy was pleased, and reopened the doors to them.

Through long evening hours, as I sat outside the village, these childlike stories seemed alive in the breeze. Their spirit, after the lashing gusts and thunder, filled the cool air with evening sweetness. The Dourdou, deep below, flowed stilly toward the silence of the sunset. And while the leaves of a cherry danced overhead, and the plumes of a locust tree fingered the air, the pink horizon faded to soft green. Lightly toward the west a whitish cloud swirled, above Conques and the higher cross-crowned height, ever upward through a sky of China blue. And the distant sweetness of sheep-bells sounded faintly in the air as the flock tinkled homeward, toward the shrine of Sainte Foy.

So night came, and with it the plaint of peasant songs. Again the sun rose. And while its shadows still stretched far down the steep, I met Sainte Foy's Spanish servant beside the church.

"Would I view the treasury now?" he asked; and he led me into a simple house.

There, one by one, he opened the mere

# Plains and Uplands of Old France

wooden cases that protect a wonderful array
of gold and silverware, embroideries and
Byzantine enamel work — a treasure, in fact,
of astounding importance. For here is a gold
reliquary of the ninth century, barbarically
wrought and set with great stones; here are
gold crosses, inlaid plates, and a box of Sainte
Foy's bones which is ornamented with exquisite
dull enamels of birds and griffins; here again is
a portable altar of eight centuries ago, whose
harmonious enamels, set in silver, surround a
slab of Oriental alabaster. In short, here is
bewildering richness on richness of material,
and in workmanship a strange mixture of skill
and crudity that draws one back to the aspiring barbarism of the early ages.

Open, then, to the spirit of those days, I
followed the Spaniard to the arch treasure of
Conques, a small mysterious statue of Sainte
Foy. Seated on her throne, and stretching
both arms stiffly forward, the rigid golden
being gazed at us through fixed eyes that made

her whole face solemn and haunting. An Eastern god, she seemed, stolen by Christians and by them decorated with that dazzling encrustation of amethysts and sapphires, cameos, pearls and uncut emeralds. Yet very strangely this pagan sumptuousness, contradicted only by two worn Christian carvings on the robe, enclosed relics of Sainte Foy, the Gaulish martyr who had dared proclaim to the Romans, "All your Gods are devils!"

But as I stood before the barbaric figure, the Spaniard interrupted thoughts which it seemed he must have guessed. "She is stern," he said. "See, this little statue is far more like her." And he pointed to a charming silver figure of the fifteenth century, Sainte Foy softened and made tender by four hundred years of dreaming, Sainte Foy simple and gracious, the very maiden whom her Spaniard loved. For surely it was this Sainte Foy, and not another, who had raised pious donkeys from the dead, and begged from her human worshippers jewels and golden doves.

"Do not forget her," he said, as on the way out we passed into a room hung with tapestries ; and he would have talked of her.

Now, however, there entered a full-fed, somewhat masterful priest who gave me a suave greeting, but sharply upbraided the Spaniard.

"Why, this floor has not been swept at all, there is dust everywhere, everywhere," he vociferated.

Sainte Foy's perhaps incompetent servant slunk away like a beaten dog; and the priest talked to me of the tapestries, specially of ones representing Lazarus and the three Marys, faring in their little boat toward Provence.

There, the priest explained, they had arrived in spite of a great storm. So Martha had tamed the terrible Tarasque, and Mary Magdalen had lived in penitence at La Sainte

Beaume near which, at Saint Maximin, her relics were still preserved.

"What?" I asked, "at Saint Maximin? But a monk brought her body to Vézelay."

"No, not at all," he exclaimed. "Do not believe it. That Vézelay legend has been refuted by several bishops."

"But," said I "at Vézelay ———"

"I do not like discussion. I believe, and that's the end of it," the priest retorted.

This statement, so perfectly typical of self-indulgent faith, stifled our conversation. We parted in mere mutual tolerance; and I rejoined the Spaniard outside.

Again he talked of Sainte Foy and of her miracles, then of a monk who had gained the confidence of the abbot at Agen where her body then rested, and had stolen it and brought it over the hills to Conques.

"But that was wrong!" the New Englander in me asserted.

"No," said he. "Such things were often

# Plains and Uplands of Old France

done in those days; and Popes have blessed our abbey. What is more, Sainte Foy herself was pleased by the removal. And when those who carried her rested on the hill, there, she made a spring burst forth to refresh them. Look! under that white cross, you can almost see it, still singing of the miracle."

Then while we slowly left the village, he strayed into talk of the hell-mouth, of other mouths like it that *monsieur le curé* said had gulped down living actors in the miracle plays, finally of a Passion play that the peasants act at Easter on the cross-crowned hillock that we saw below us.

"You must come back and see it," he said, and as we came to the bend in the road, we shook hands.

So forgetting the hell-mouth above the portal, and remembering only the indulgent sweetness of Sainte Foy and her humble Spaniard, I returned into the valley. Again in Marcillac, I slept at the pretty hunchback's inn, and

# Plains and Uplands of Old France

woke ; came higher past Rodez, and by gradual stages nearer to the Cévennes till in Mende, at last, I reached the border of bright uplands where spirits of gayety bestride the winds.

# Plains and Uplands of Old France

## A BOATING SONG

*AH, lightly blowing her amber hair,*
*Jewelled with drops of spray,*
*Dances and turns in summer air*
*While whirling my soul away.*

*But though in hope the resplendent sun*
*Gayly her lips may greet,*
*My hope, alas, undone, undone,*
*Lies dead at her bare brown feet.*

# Plains and Uplands of Old France

## THROUGH A LAND OF THE BIZARRE

N sunlight which made the thin haze luminous, a stretch of wheat fields below Mende glowed with the richly rippling orange of a river at dusk. But high in the mid-day air hills oddly more inviting rose, beyond the gray little town, like mammoth earthworks ; and down from the heights a breeze blew so freshly that it filled me with the wish to be off, upward.

So off I drove in a sort of elongated buggy ; and a spare peasant perched in front shared and prodded my delight.

"Already one finds the air lighter ! Isn't that so," he asked, as we trotted along the deep valley of the Lot. Again after half an hour of plodding silence, " One is happy here," he exclaimed, " Isn't that so ? One enjoys life ! " Then pointing across the ravine that dropped into steep depths beside us he showed

# Plains and Uplands of Old France

me, on the opposite height, a lion-shaped great rock. "He is pretty from here," this blithe driver remarked; "and from further on there, he is still prettier. But look, on the next hill there's another. Do you see his paws? One might almost think he'd been made so on purpose."

Soon, now, we had finished the ascent; and trotting along a nearly level road we looked back along the lowland. But the rolling plain which we had reached lifted its rough edge above them, and as we advanced seemed to reach back farther and farther till it merged into the half-seen blue of the Aubrac Mountains and the Margéride. Then our table-land, the Causse de Severac as it is called, revealed itself at last as it really is, not a series of rampart-like hills rising from fields of wheat, but a bleakly elevated, undulating upland in which the valleys are mere sabre-slashes. The deep Lot was lost behind us; and ahead, the sharp cut of the Tarn was not yet visible. The

# Plains and Uplands of Old France

treeless land, covered with short-cropped grass and wild thyme, stretched its dull greenness forward monotonous and drear, except where some tiny field at the bottom of a hollow shone like an emerald in the sun.

"Yep — u!" the driver crooned in a gentle falsetto; and we trotted on between strange hillocks that lay along the near horizon like inverted saucers. "Yep — u!" he crooned again, more to express delight in the rare high air than to hurry his horse. And on we jogged while to the left, red circular hills, topped with white, raised the sharp contrast of their color slowly into the dark blue sky.

"One would say it had snowed," remarked the driver. As I looked at the hill-tops, I could almost believe that their whiteness was snow lying there, miraculously unmelted, in the August sunshine. For now everything around us was perverse. On all sides the bare land was so red that its staring desolation made the few distant little trees seem dark gray. An

# Plains and Uplands of Old France

expanse of dead monotonous brown, broken by only the black stones that cropped out here and there, stretched upward before us to the near horizon. And beyond, one could see and imagine — nothing. It seemed the end of the world.

But cheerily the driver crooned, "Yep — u!" For him mere desolateness could not conquer the exhilaration of the air and blinding afternoon sun. And as we neared the seeming final edge of things he pointed to a faint blueness that rose into the void, became the waves of a great sea, then, as we gained the crest of the slope, resolved itself suddenly into the more material, immovable waves of a mountain range, a range of the surging blue Cévennes.

"We're not on this earth! That's a landscape in the moon!" I exclaimed.

The driver drew up short, and answered, with a self-contained droll smile, "At least we may call it hunchbacked France!"

# Plains and Uplands of Old France

Then down, down we drove again with a
yellow, finger-topped height across the ravine
on our left, and beyond, as we came near the
Tarn, blue gaps of valley opening further and
further toward Florac and the tracks of highland Stevenson and his donkey, Modestine.
Memories of them tugged, in friendly fashion,
at my mind.  Almost they persuaded me to
follow the sweet vagabond's footsteps.  But
my driver, with his quiet calls or caution to
the horse, brought my thoughts back to the
Tarn which, near us  now, turned  the road
from Florac on  the left, and away into an opposite cleft.

All yellow with the stain  of recent storms
the river flowed swift between bleak banks.
Across it a piney steep climb  through shadows to a precipice that reared its black body
against  the  face  of  the  sun.   And  on  this
side, from  the  foot  of a sky-invading cliff
above us, loose stone seemed  ever  on  the
point of slipping past the nut trees dotted

# Plains and Uplands of Old France

here and there, down over the long gray slides, and across the road to the river. But even through the storms those hesitant masses had remained unmoved — only earth and some gravel had been washed loose and away; and the lank course of that, lying straight down the steep bare slope, seemed trivial, artificial, a mere leather strap.

"Comic," the driver dubbed it; and cracked his whip defiantly.

As we trotted forward, however, the Tarn fell beneath the nearly level road, little by little, into impressive depths. It flowed in a cañon, now. From above a wall of rock we saw only its further side and rising high above it a second river-wall, a precipice pierced at half its height by two waterfalls which gush from the rock into air and tumble past a little stone mill, into the river.

"See," said the driver, pointing to the green streak that their pure subterranean waters made in the troubled Tarn, "See, that is the true color of the river — green like the trees."

But now all colors began to merge into dusk. Though we stood in brightness, the opposite slope rose very dark toward the zenith. From above the high horizon the sun threw a slanting line of light across the valley; and as we drove on, the shining shaft slanted less and less. Before us, in the roughly V-shaped cleft, the tide of shadow mounted till all but the tower of a castle, just now aglow with sunshine, was dark. Then we too were cut off. And still the great shadow rose. We went down into yet duskier depths. And as we descended, the shaft of light sloped gently and more gently till at last, full sixteen hundred feet above us, it lit only the topmost rocks with its rays of horizontal gold.

In darkness we drove into Sainte Enemie. But lights shone out through the windows of

# Plains and Uplands of Old France

its hostelry; and as we entered, their cheer was heightened to gayety by a brisk uncorking of bottles.

"To our friendship" the driver proposed; and we clinked glasses, and hastily drank down our beer.

Still vigorous then, next day, his friendship abode with me — by proxy. Though he himself was jogging homeward, two boatmen in blue blouses and corduroy trousers, were waiting when I came out into the reflected light of the dawn far above; and as they gave me his "good day" and their own, a peasant woman and her pretty little girl appeared.

"They will go along part way, if *monsieur* doesn't mind," said one of the boatmen.

So when, with a nod of agreement, I had seated myself half way down the oblong scow, my self-invited guests seated themselves beside a ladder and a basket; and as the men, one in the "bow," one aft, poled us silently into the current, and down the cleft-like valleys the peasant woman began to chat.

"*Ecouta mé!*" She said, and rushed on through a maze of patois that doubtless was most picturesque, for the little girl opened wide eyes. But "What does she say?" I was forced to ask.

So the boatman behind me retold in French his uncouth, vigorous tale of the rains and the floods which, only three days before, had carried trees and even cows down toward the rapids. And while he talked, the now peaceful Tarn carried us steadily forward. It turned, and a morning shadow fell chill across the water. Then the sun flashed out again, strewing half the stream with quicksilver while the still shaded half, reflecting the sky and the trees, rippled on, blue as lapis-lazuli, and emerald-green, so strangely bright indeed that the peasant child began to dabble her hands among its seeming jewels.

"*Tranquillo!*" said the boatman forward.

# Plains and Uplands of Old France

But she and I had begun a splashing battle. *" Tranquillo! Tranquillo! "* he repeated, and menaced her with his pole.

Motionless, then, she sat silent and subdued, all but her eyes which gleamed under the black, spray-bejewelled hair; they glanced defiantly hither and thither along the dark shore, halted, shifted again and fixed themselves at last on a point far forward. We drew near, and soon were poled to the very spot. The old woman stepped from the boat, and stood with her basket on her arm, uttering her thanks in patois. The girl gave me a shake of the hand, then leaned forward for a childlike kiss, but thought better of it, and jumped suddenly to the bank. And when I had tossed the ladder after her, both mother and daughter set off with many a smile to scale the steep and gather their basketful of berries.

Forward sped the Tarn, and fast as we followed, it led still faster down through the green, deep valley. But where, I wondered, were the gulfs and huge precipices of which a peasant had told me? Beyond the next turn, perhaps? But there the valley, though narrow and very steep, was wooded still.

"Beyond the *next* turn?" I guessed again.

"No," said the forward boatman; "There we shall see the village of Saint Chély"; and through his brass horn he blew a long summoning blast, then half a dozen staccato toots, and again a long blast.

"That's to call new boatmen," he explained while the echoes were still singing the last note.

A rapid hurried us toward the still invisible village. With a great slapping of waves against our bow we drove straight toward a bank of precipitous red rock, abruptly turned, and from a shaded calm that was pungent with the fresh scent of boxwood, saw, just ahead, some stone houses and the waiting boatmen. I was ensconced in their scow. The first two men

# Plains and Uplands of Old France

labored upstream again. And with my new companions I drifted onward between silvery willows, poplars, and wooded slopes that rose here and there to castellated rocks, and glowed red and yellow against the summer sky.

No precipices, however, rose from the shores. As yet the Tarn ran through no dark cañons. Its sunlit waters rippled beneath the flight of darting green-winged dragon-flies. By a tiny town where we lunched, vineyards clambered along the slopes; and a road easily wriggled its way down from the *causse*. As we went on, however, the Tarn at last ran into narrows; beneath overhanging rocks it allowed us but a swift upward glance at a former cave-refuge of the Huguenots; then racing us past a fantastic natural bridge, it came out into a great circle of yellow, blue-gray and red precipices so wall-like and high that through four winter months they hide all sunlight from the river.

After hours of mere playful picturesqueness

# Plains and Uplands of Old France

the Tarn had shown itself at last almost as untamed as the peasantry describe it. But it could not remain consistent in its wildness. Capricious, rather, almost coquettish, it ran on — to its own swallowing up in a wilderness of broken rocks tossed hither and thither, and piled together in some riot of the old earth's giants ; then freeing itself again it bore me with new boatmen, boisterously on through rapids that hissed, growled and dashed spray into the scow, only to die into a placid calm where trees were reflected and where locusts buzzed drowsily in the sunshine.

Finally as we glided into the rosy light of sunset, the peaceful banks made all the past rocks and boulders seem like some half-forgotten tale. But a peak rising before us, topped with figures of deformed rock, revived the Tarn's wildness. And sportive again and wanton it dashed off as if to outdo itself, toward scenes still more bizarre.

# Plains and Uplands of Old France

## PIERRE OF PROVENCE
## TO
## MAGUELONE THE FAIR

*FAIR Maguelone,*
*Since Heaven hath swept my bark away*
*From Thee, from Thee,*
*I kneel here gazing, day by day,*
*Across the sea.*

*And dear mine own,*
*Though one as fair as Thou art dear —*
*And yet more fair ! —*
*Doth woo my heart, I hardly hear*
*Her sweet despair.*

*But Maguelone,*
*I yearn toward days beyond our death*
*When Thou and I,*
*One passionate soul, one burning breath,*
*Shall brave the sky !*

# Plains and Uplands of Old France

## MAGUELONE

S the carriage rattled along, and prosperous Montpellier gradually became a white hillock against the rugged blue Cévennes, I passed into tracts of bare yellow ground that rolled forward, on the right toward two conical hills, and on the left toward an expanse of flatness. Rows of stumpy vines, cut short, for it was winter, swung continually past; slowly the checkered land turned about a distant black poplar, windswept and bleak; then a stiff clump of umbrella pines appeared, and beside them a sunny sheltered house and solid barns telling of such patriarchal life as the poets sing in near Provence. On we trotted. The farm sank below an undulation, and on a little ridge ahead there rose an avenue of white pines and a house whose ivy-grown walls were battlemented all about, and guarded at the corners by strong old towers. As we drew near, its

# Plains and Uplands of Old France

feudalism melted into the winning calm of an aristocratic home; its charm called to me to stay. But the driver hurried relentlessly into pasture-land where shepherds, hooded and wrapped in blanket capes, watched motionless by their flocks. We crossed a little river that curved green under banks of rock, and reflected bent poplars. At last, along a road bordered with bushy live-oaks, we triumphantly rattled into a plastered little village, Villeneuve-les-Maguelonnes.

Now, unshaved and rather dazed driver to the contrary notwithstanding, Villeneuve-les-Maguelonnes seemed a name new-fangled in comparison with the Maguelone which during the middle ages had sung in the imagination of troubadours. What is more, the old village church, in spite of its primitive cross decorated with cock, nails, sponge, ladder and the other instruments of the passion, was surely not the shrine of my special pilgrimage, for in it there was no tomb ancient and

# Plains and Uplands of Old France

lovely enough to have guarded the body of Maguelone the Fair.

So I came out into sunlight again, and encouraging the desperate driver, drove off by cart-tracks leading through vineyards — nowhere. I eagerly listened to sundry discussions in the local patois, an illegitimate vague relative of Provençal; then took a northerly tack; and at last, looking back from raised ground to a sudden shimmering vision of the Mediterranean, I saw on a long bent arm of sand, a company of pines and in their midst a heavy stone mass.

" Maguelone ! " I exclaimed, pointing out the former cathedral.

" That is merely some country church," the driver answered.

But at a farm-house where we stopped for further patois parleyings, it turned out that I was right.

" Poor Maguelone," thought I, as finally we turned toward her church eastward through

# Plains and Uplands of Old France

the marshes, "poor Maguelone!" For her story, though once written in sweet Provençal and written again in German, English, and even Arabic, seemed less widely remembered than the story of Gérard de Rousillon or the story of Roland; and she was almost unknown even in this salt region where Bernard de Treviers, sang her life-long love.

Maguelone, daughter of the Prince of Naples, was very fair to see. This I rediscovered as the carriage rumbled along and I turned the leaves of "Pierre de Provence et la belle Maguelone." And the prince her father gave in her honor a great tournament to which rode Pierre, son of the Count of Provence, drawn by the fame of her great beauty and very eager to prove his valor before her. And that she might judge him by his deeds alone and not according to his rank, he arrayed himself in white armor, and kept his visor closed, and on his shield he bore no arms but two golden keys, the emblem of his patron, Saint Peter who holds the keys of heaven. Therefore he was known only as "the Knight of the Keys," and under this name he fought valiantly, and overbore all other knights in the lists, so that fair Maguelone marveled at his prowess, and gladly rose to crown him. But first she begged that he would remove his helmet, which doing he discovered to her a face so comely and gentle and so strong withal that she loved him with her whole heart.

But their love, alas, must needs pass through many and sore trials. For after he had carried her away from a very fierce suitor it happened that, weary with journeying, she lay in a wood, asleep. And while she slept, a bird of prey seized upon three golden rings which Pierre had received from his mother, and which now he had given Maguelone. Wherefore when the bird flew out over the waters, he followed in a small boat. And being attacked by a sudden great storm and driven hither and thither among the black waves, he

# Plains and Uplands of Old France

fell at last into the hands of corsairs who sold him to the Sultan of Egypt. Him he served. And though he suffered continually, weeping in his soul for Maguelone, he was so diligent that he attained the Sultan's highest favor and great promises of recompense even to half the riches of Egypt. But he would take no recompense except only liberty; and resisting all temptation, even the love of a woman so like his beloved that in truth it seemed she stood before him, he left Egypt; and again passed over the sea; and at last, worn and wellnigh desperate, came to the hospital of Saint Peter.

There a lay sister received him sweetly, washing his feet and weeping while he told her of his suffering and love. And in his despair she comforted him, saying: "Maguelone is alive; and though, as she lay sleeping in the wood, you seemed to have deserted her, still she is full of trust. For your sake she has founded this hospital; and laboring here she awaits her beloved." Then raising her veil the sister asked him : " If now she stood before you would you know her ? "

So they embraced one another, pressing lips against lips and heart against heart. And thus Pierre of Provence was joined again to Maguelone the Fair, forever.

With the tender story living before my eyes I rattled almost blindly along the shore of the shallow bay. Still close to the gleaming water and salt-whitened marsh-grasses, I and my driver turned out into a narrow peninsula through the midst of which, on our left, the little river Lez sped between bay and bay toward the sea. We followed past a rowboat tugging at its anchor, past a curved line of corks marking a net across stream, on, on to an oddly Dutch-looking village, Palavas-les-Flots where wooden, red, blue, and green houses tempted us, from each side of the stream, with many a painted offer of *bouilla-*

*baisse.* But we resisted these appetising allurements; and turning our back on the picturesqueness of the net-strewn river banks, dragged through a reach of sand. On our right, bending pampas-grasses separated a long stretch of sand-vineyard from the bay; on the left, a rampart of sand protected the narrow vineyard from the sea. And along the arm of sand a road, bordered with short vapory-topped tamarisks, led us slowly toward the dark hillock where Maguelone stands eternally among the pines.

Through the soughing of the wind about an ancient cross, we came up past empty stone coffins among the tree-trunks, and halted in sunlight. Then two steps, and beyond some cacti we saw suddenly a precipitous low hill of stone, the Cathedral. Stirred by its enormous dumbness I stood still and thought of great souls who had prayed there, Saint Roch and Saint Dominic, Guy of the Order of the Holy Ghost, and a sweet spirit lately in the flesh.

# Plains and Uplands of Old France

And silent under its heavy huge gray sides I dreamt of how faithfully this fief of the Holy See had withstood the Saracens; I imagined the former city living about it, and mourned over the day when the Cathedral lamps were quenched after ten centuries of worship, and when the winds from the encircling sea began slowly to bury the altar in sand.

But as I started along the gravel path, prettily placed shrubs showed that Maguelone was no longer deserted. For many years, in fact, the cathedral had been a private chapel. And it was dearly loved, said a smiling wrinkled fat peasant woman whom I called from the patriarchal midday meal of " monsieur's " retainers.

Certainly she had cause to cherish it, I thought as she unlocked the little door in the blank front wall of the church. For here, carved very skillfully, were curious quaint bas-reliefs in yellowish and blushing marble; above the doorway the Father surrounded by

# Plains and Uplands of Old France

His symbolic Angel, Lion, Ox and Eagle; on the lintel clear-cut almost classical leafage; to the left of the doorway, Saint Paul kneeling; and on the right, Saint Peter, patron of Pierre de Provence.

The door swung open; and I passed between the saint of the sword and the saint of the keys into a dark gulf of tenderness that fills the spirit with awe. Even the driver, as he came in, gazed reverently through the dimness toward a vault that arched ponderously low from wall to wall; and taking off his *sabots* he muttered, "Men who have not seen this have seen nothing," then, "It will endure as long as the world is the world."

With that he followed me from under the low vault. We glanced back to the chapel above it. And looking forward again into the higher vault and the half-dome of the apse we worshipped their calmness. They circled over all with strength huge enough to bear the sorrow of centuries. They were succoring,

not austere. And the whole church filled me
with a growing sense of its kindness. As we
came toward the altar four stone bishops, resting on their tombs, beckoned me back to their
ancient benevolent care. A sarcophagus,
broken and empty but rich with interlaced
carving, carried me into the loveliest days of
chivalry ; for Maguelone the Fair had slept in
its hollow after her life's end. And trust and
love equal to hers welcomed me to the opposite transept where, as the peasant woman
affectionately said, "Monsieur's" daughter
used to pray, and where lilies and roses glad-
den her sweet grave.

I would have stayed long among these
flowers ; but the old woman's *sabots* clicked
on the flagging somewhat impatiently. She
insisted on showing six grim skulls of bishops ;
she bade us admire a fine old painting with
which a deputy of Louis XIII had been bribed
not to destroy the castle ; she led us through a

# Plains and Uplands to Old France

little door near the tomb of Maguelone, up
a straight staircase in the thickness of the wall
to a wooden outside landing among the ivy-
clad ruins, then in again to the upper chapel.

There the driver was seized with a mania for
climbing. While I looked down into the silent
apse he scrambled to narrow slits overlooking
the sea; and with wide-eyed delight he exam-
ined the opening through which the defenders
of the church used to pour down boiling
water on visitors who, as the peasant woman
said, "did not suit them." When I had finished examining the rusted crozier of the
bishops of Maguelone, he followed eagerly up
again through the wall to the gently sloping
stone roof. "Ah, here one feels free," he
exclaimed; and he clambered about the stumpy
tower and cut himself a branching stick on
which to mount two birds; for by avocation,
as he said, he was a taxidermist.

Meantime I gloried in wind from the two
conical hills that we had seen as we drove.

# Plains and Uplands of Old France

With glance fixed on the sunny southern sea, I thought of Charles Martel, conqueror of the seafaring Saracens. Eyeing the dark blue waters and the sand-reaches eastward, I half hoped to spy Aigues-Mortes whence Saint Louis had set sail for Palestine. And thus inspired with the mystic and warlike spirit of the Mediterranean I descended again, through stone formed of its sand and dead shells, toward the tender darkness of the church.

Following the old woman, who took off her *sabots* so as to feel her way with her feet, we came through the midst of the wall, back to the landing among ivy-covered ruins, then further downward and to the tomb of Maguelone the Fair. We stood a moment in the apse, against the deep red hangings of which gleamed a silver pine on a blue ground, the shield of Maguelone. We passed among the four stone bishops at rest on their tombs. We breathed the perfume of lilies and roses;

and at last went slowly out between Saint Peter and Saint Paul.

For our farewell to this feudal home of the spirit the peasant woman led me by a path around a clump of trees to an isolated building, "monsieur's" study. I might go in, she said, for "monsieur" was at Montpelier; had been there ever since the vintage. So I boldly entered, — and saw a brightly-lighted little Gothic chapel, its sides lined with bookshelves, and the bare stone of the apse and the west end hung with two framed illuminations and a few photographs, among them one of the fortified pilgrimage church of the "Saintes-Maries de la Mer."

In this study "monsieur" — Frédéric Fabrège — had lived with ecclesiastical works, the classics, and Rousseau, Leibnitz, Kant, and Hegel. Here, close to the great church where the Eternal lives eternally, he had labored year after year on its holy war-racked history.

# Plains and Uplands of Old France

And seated at this table he had written these words on his daughter, the mystical sweet spirit whose tomb had given his sea-girt home its most intimate sacredness :

She "grew up among us, in the shadow of these walls, like a lily in the midst of ruins. Her heart, continually lifted toward God, was always fascinated by thought of supernatural things." During an illness that held her nailed to her bed from childhood, she rejoiced in the pain which "united her to Christ crucified." And so at last "she suddenly seemed to be born again, still more beautiful, more radiant, more living. In tones of unspeakable loveliness, she bade farewell to her parents, her friends and her servants; filled with a new spirit, illuminated already with the light of infinity, transfigured in an ecstacy of divine love, she spoke words that shook those about her. And thus, without pain, and smiling with the enchanted smile of the angels, she gave back her soul to the Creator."

# Plains and Uplands of Old France

## THE HOLY PEAK

*FAR down this sharp sheer precipice, alone*
*In cavern-depths, poor passionate Magdalen*
*Wept, through repentant years, a tender rain*
*Which formed the ever-flowing rill Huveaune.*
*But in the darkness Michael heard her moan,*
*And drove the torturing demons forth amain*
*Before his dazzling sword while from all pain.*
*Soaring bright angels bore her to this stone.*

*Wrapped in her golden wind-tossed hair she knelt,*
*Here amid incense of wild thyme, to Him*
*Whom she loved much: her tear-filled eyes,*
*still dim,*
*Beheld the storm-wind's waning tumult cease;*
*She saw His coming, and her wild heart felt*
*The calm sweet joy of His eternal peace.*

# Plains and Uplands of Old France

## A PILGRIMAGE TO THE PAST

"WAKE UP! seven o'clock, seven, seven!" growled mine host.

"Yes," I murmured from amid my sleepy reminiscences of Mary Magdalen's bones; for I was in the village of Saint Maximin, her resting-place.

"Are you up?" insisted my mentor.

"Yes, yes," I answered.

And to clear myself of the lie, I threw off blankets, spread, overcoats, everything that had allayed my shivering; and tiptoed across the tiles. Slipping into chilly clothes I looked out over a frost-whitened field to hills dark under the brilliant dawn; then trotted down stairs; ensconced myself as near the kitchen fire as cat and kettles would allow; and sat thinking of the village church and its treasure of ancient green and golden embroideries, till a toothless old woman in cap and apron led me to the dining-room and a bowl of goat's

# Plains and Uplands of Old France

milk coffee which, as she said, was "so hot and so good."

Warm, then, and fortified after a fashion by most of a loaf, I soon hunted up the driver, and after "au revoirs" to mine host and the petulant cat, drove through a street or two into open country.

There, still in sight of the towerless great village church, we passed through the long frosty shadow of a pillar that bears aloft a battered carving.

"See! the two angels flying with Sainte Madelaine to Saint Maximin where she died!" said the driver. "And look," he went on, pointing to a height far ahead, "there is Lou Sant Pieloun (The Holy Peak) where they used to carry her to pray."

" — as Mistral says," I added.

To my Provençal driver, however, Mistral meant only the rough North Wind whose name the poet so undeservedly bears. The legends, however, and the rural life that Mis-

# Plains and Uplands of Old France

tral loves were familiarly dear to his country-
man. He talked confidently of Sainte
Madelaine, and while we drove between
glistening olive trees, he described the pressing of the olives so gladly and so vividly that
forgotten scenes from " Mireillo," shining
again in my memory, mingled their sunshine
with the morning mist and the whiteness of
the frost that lay like snow in the shadow of
each tree.

But as we trotted on through a rolling
country strewn with brown volcanic stones,
our conversation turned ; and the driver, suddenly drear as the few stiff cypresses about us,
talked distressfully of politics. Royalists,
Bonapartists, Socialists, all politicians were
equally selfish, all equally corrupt. None really
cared for the people. And what could the
people do? Nothing—except to work along,
every man for himself, till called on to revenge
the country against Prussia.

But now the Holy Peak, before this

# Plains and Uplands of Old France

but one among a range of distant hills, was
rising high and near, between us and the unseen Mediterranean. Other heights, growing
as it grew, closed in around us. By the roadside, gray heather and a few yellow-tufted
pines filled the sunlight with highland scents.
And when, at last, we had passed beyond the
little village of Nans and a feudal castle in
ruins, pine woods made all the air about us
fresh with shaded sweetness.

Trudging beside the carriage as it jostled
up the wood-road, we found the frozen ruts
strewn with pine-needles and brown leaves ;
and these, like the green leaves of each wayside holly, were frost-encrusted with silvery crystal-work. Fallen twigs lay thinly
shrouded, as if in some tissue of frozen
bluish smoke. The very rocks, white, gray
and red, were veiled with the silent and magic
breath of cold. But as we turned a corner
upward into the sunshine, both rocks and
branches glared like silver, and the leaves

here and there glistened with jewels of melted frost, first green, then yellow, then orange and fiery red.

Through a sparkling wonderland, then, we came gladly beyond the woods and found ourselves climbing along a bushy steep. Green with laurels and boxwood, it fell on our right, lower and yet lower; and turning ahead of us it closed the narrow valley. There, beneath perpendicular rocks, our road also turned. We crossed a little brook; and making our way around mountain-flank that was striped among its bushes with curving ribs of stone, we climbed on till the hills westward fell low into a lake of brown mist, and the level wind brought us, from across its surface, keen draughts of the upper air.

A moment more, and we were trotting along the flat upland where Dominicans, those "Dogs of the Lord," stand on guard below Mary Magdalen's cave. Seemingly untenanted, however, the plain stretched indefinitely

# Plains and Uplands of Old France

toward arid distances, except on our left where the Holy Peak rose in a long precipice toward the sun. Before us, however, vague wheel-tracks led the way to a low wall in the middle of which a gate stood open. We entered. And to the right and the left of the enclosed yard we found a stable and the monks' silent, stone hospice.

" There," said the driver, pointing toward the hospice door.

I pulled the bell-handle : inside there was a shrill echoing tinkle, then a light sound of steps ; and as the door opened, a black-robed, ruddy sister answered my request for a meal.

Yes, she said quietly, if I would wait an hour I might have lunch before climbing to La Sainte Baume. And with hardly another word she showed me to a cold bare room.

It was solitary and very still. In the fire-place a few branches and twigs sparked weakly, and sputtered. Only reflected light entered the window opposite. At one end of the room

# Plains and Uplands of Old France

disused chairs were piled up homelessly, and the yellowish walls were prison-like around. But a little notice hanging near the door explained so gently how hard it was to provide comforts or even food in this inaccessible region, that I was touched, even while laughing at the apologetic price-list that followed. Fifty *sous*, for example, seemed so pathetically unsuccessful as an extortionate charge for lunch! Accordingly the monks' kind *naïveté* gave charm to their excuses, and their simple spirit grew evident throughout the room. Two harmless water colors which softened the asceticism of the walls, gained a certain sweetness. The ivory crucifix and the print of Mary Magdalen that stood beside it on the mantel, lost their crudeness in the sincerity of faith; and as time flowed imperceptibly away, their symbolic beauty gradually transfused even the faded faltering music which somewhere in the distance was accompanying mass.

Silence fell. Soon, however, a bell struck

# Plains and Uplands of Old France

twelve, and its singing lingered in the still-
ness, moment after moment, till a quick step
drew near, and a black-caped, youthful monk
with a blue apron over the front of his white
robe and with blue sleeves drawn over its arms,
stood before me in the doorway.

" Monsieur's lunch is ready," he somewhat
shyly announced; and silent again, brought me
through a passage, past an instant's glimpse of
flowers on a window-sill, then a few steps
further to just such a cell as Fra Angelico's in
Florence.

Tiny and white-washed and square, it lacked
only the frail fresco to be his. And though
that almost angelic charm was denied it, the
monk, pulling aside a curtain before the small
high window, gave it that golden beauty of
mountain sunlight which, as he said, makes
the heart joyous.

So with his rosary clicking as he went, he
strode to the kitchen; and soon back again,
set on the small bare table, wine, bread, and a

# Plains and Uplands of Old France

bowl of *pot au feu*; then eggs fried in olive oil; then cheese; a homely meal in short, but so bountiful that I lingered long and at the last was quite willing to pay the full price.

" No," said the monk, " it is too much. It must not be thought of. You have had no meat!"

Expostulation was useless. Even forty *sous*, he felt sure, was too much. Considering the poverty of the monastery, however, he accepted that; and as if I were some benefactor of the brotherhood accompanied me out of doors, and some steps toward the forest.

The limbs and twigs of huge ivy-grown oaks threw a covering of shadow-lace on the leaves that whispered underfoot. But the holly-bushes, almost trees in the open forest, glinted cheerily in the rare shafts of sun-shine; their red berries still glowed gayly as I sauntered toward the unbroken shadows of the precipice; and on the limbs of a bare great

# Plains and Uplands of Old France

beech, sprigs of mistletoe, white-berried and pale, gave the surrounding wintriness a touch of the Christmas spirit.

Gray and cold, however, the precipice now appeared among the branches ; and the path, after mounting by slow zig-zags to its foot, turned sharply aside and led me clambering, over loose stones and bare white rocks, up and out of the forest, above the tree-tops and ever higher till only a ridge of rock barred me from the sky.

Three steps more, and in the uplifting wind of heaven I stood looking down an expanse of whiteness, bright and translucent as ghostly snow. Smooth and silvery, an ocean of placid mist, it shone beneath the lower breeze, unruffled except where a few waves tossed moveless above the high horizon and where two islets of mist shone against the sky like dazzling icebergs.

With steep olive-slopes dipping far below me into the veiled splendor, I climbed on over rocks and wild thyme; and where the precipice falls deep into the forest I came at last to the highest height. There on the Holy Peak where the angels had brought Mary Magdalen day by day to worship God, I turned from the Alps which rose snow-capped and jagged into the northern sky, and gazing westward saw the far hill of Notre Dame de la Garde above the bishopric of Lazarus, then facing again to the south looked long through the sea of mist to where the sun made a vague golden path on the second and lower sea, the Mediterranean among whose holy waves Lazarus and the three Marys had fared miraculously to Provence.

The sun's glory waned; and as the shadow of the Holy Peak stirred beneath me among more and more distant tree-tops, night threatened the valley. So I turned from the precipice, and hurried along the ridge to the steep path. With the wonderful perfume

# Plains and Uplands of Old France

of wild thyme still sweet in my nostrils, I ran helter-skelter down over rocks and small white stones. Trees darted their black branches across the whiteness of the Alps and darkened the sky with a mesh-work of twigs. Again, as I ran, the cold gray precipice rose higher and higher above the trees. Then, at a turn in the path, steps suddenly appeared, climbing to a stone platform against the face of the mountain; for there, as I soon found, was the entrance to Mary Magdalen's cave.

Through a little door in a wall that seemed part of the precipice itself, I came into sub-terranean grayness. Standing beneath the unhewn vault of rock I peered past a white altar into deep darkness where, men say, the suffering saint wept and prayed. And as I looked, these legends, sacred through the be-lief of centuries, seemed to mingle with the quiet sound of water falling drop by drop into the spring where the rill of her tears was born; and mingling thus, they seemed to sing on forever in its slow, sweet irregular song.

At last from the cave and the forest of oaks and holly I came again to the upland plain. With a word to a wandering white-robed monk, my friend the lover of God's sunshine, I came on toward the monastery; and there found the driver waiting, his carriage bedecked with green.

"Does that annoy monsieur?" he asked as I looked. "I gathered it to show where we have been. It grows nowhere else."

So bearing with us this trophy of the Holy Peak where the spirit of old France still lives, we drove again toward Saint Maximin and that modern democratic France which struggles on in the hope of such justice and liberty as are not yet.

*Of this first Edition of the* Plains and Uplands of Old France *by Henry Copley Greene with title-page, initials and two full-page decorations drawn by George H. Hallowell, seven hundred and fifty copies have been printed at the Heintzemann Press in Boston, during December, 1898, for Small, Maynard & Company of Boston.*